HER NOT SO EMPTY NEST
Golden Gate Romance Series, Book Five

BARBARA MCMAHON

1

"Goodbye. Be happy," Ashley Bennett called after the festively decorated car as it drove down the curving driveway from the high-rise hotel, tin cans clanking behind it. One of their friends had written Just Married with foam on all the windows. Another had painted hearts and cupids. Another had tied ribbons from the door handles and antenna, all gaily fluttering in the wind.

She watched until the vehicle was out of sight, feeling a sudden pang. It'd happened too fast. Charlie had come home on temporary duty after a year and a half assignment on a Naval ship in the Med. He and Michelle told her only last week they were getting married. Now the deed was done.

Her baby was married and off to start her new life with a husband who only had another month at most in the States before being deployed again for another sea assignment.

The wedding had been small, only family and a few close, longtime friends of the bride and groom. The young men and women who had gathered to celebrate the event cheered as the newlyweds drove off. Now they were leaving.

One of Michelle's friends came to give Ashley a hug.

"Super wedding, wasn't it?" she said.

Ashley nodded, wishing it had been so different.

"Seems like they're still kids to me," Phyllis Stratford said coming to stand beside Ashley.

The two women watched the other young people drift away. The mother of the groom didn't look any happier about things than Ashley felt.

"They're still kids. Michelle's only nineteen," Ashley said, trying not to feel defensive.

Michelle was a year older than Ashley had been when she married. Of course, look how that had turned out.

She shivered a little in the cold air. The sun shone from a cloudless sky, but the February temperatures at Lake Tahoe were still below freezing. Snow blanketed the surrounding mountains—a skier's paradise. And a favorite location for weddings.

"Charlie's twenty-one, and two years already into his enlistment. After he gets out, he'll have the G.I. Bill to help with college," Phyllis said.

She'd put her coat on and stood looking a bit lost.

If he'd apply himself. Ashley knew better than to suggest any criticism of Phyllis' only child. He was the apple of her eye. Ashley had known her for years, ever since Michelle and Charlie had begun dating while in high school. They'd had their spats over the years, but remained loyal to each other despite everything.

Charlie, however, had never struck Ashley as particularly ambitious.

Michelle had bemoaned the fact Charlie was a year ahead of her in school, wanting to graduate at the same time. She hadn't liked the fact he'd joined the U.S. Navy upon graduation, but she remained loyal and steadfast, even when he'd been posted overseas.

Now this. Ashley wasn't sure they were making a mistake.

There were many couples who married young and subsequently celebrated fifty years of happy married life.

She only wished they'd waited. Michelle had started her second year of college, while Charlie was posted overseas. She hoped Michelle wouldn't throw away her chance at finishing her education to go live on a Navy base to be closer to him.

She knew the two of them had discussed it. The last she heard, Michelle planned to finish the school year in San Francisco. They wanted to see where Charlie would be assigned next before making further plans.

She wished they'd waited that extra year instead of rushing things along. But they were grown and none of her comments had them even reconsidering their impetuous decision.

Ashley's own experiences colored everything, she knew. She'd married young, like Michelle. She and her husband had been childhood sweethearts, like Michelle and Charlie. Yet Darrell had deserted her and Michelle when Michelle was three months old.

There'd been no college for Ashley at age nineteen. No husband with a good job. Not even a support network to help.

Her parents had turned their backs when she'd married against their wishes. Darrell's parents had been equally unavailable. Alone, and with a baby to support, Ashley had grown up fast. Those first few years had been so hard.

But worth every moment because of Michelle. Her daughter was the apple of *her* eye.

She smiled at Phyllis.

"I wish they were still little kids who listened to us without question, but they're both adults now, and embarking on life's journey together. Once they have a college education, the world will be at their feet."

She crossed her arms over her chest, hugging what warmth she could. She had to get inside or freeze to death.

"They could have waited," Phyllis said with a sigh.

"I agree, but they didn't. They're young, in love, and have been dating exclusively for years," Ashley said.

She could say she blamed Charlie for rushing the wedding through, but she refrained. No sense starting off with bad feelings with her new in-laws.

"Leave it alone, Phyllis," Samuel Stratford said, joining them. "The boy knows what he's doing." He looked at Ashley. "Are you heading back to the city now?"

He was a heavy-set man who ruled his family with no questions asked. Ashley was never completely comfortable around him, though he'd always been friendly enough.

She hoped Charlie didn't try to rule his family so totally. She had a feeling Michelle wouldn't put up with it like Phyllis did.

Ashley relished her own independence and it seemed to her as if Phyllis was always bowing her wishes to her husband's.

"I'm staying on for a couple of days. I took a week off," she said in response to Samuel's question.

Since she'd come up two days ago to help with the final touches of the wedding, she still had several days remaining of her vacation. And she wanted to maximize every second.

It was already the first of February–tax season had begun. By the time April rolled around, she'd be putting in long hours to get taxes completed for many of the company's clients. The busiest time of year for accountants was about to begin. She was going to do her best to enjoy the lull before the onslaught.

Ashley bid the Stratfords goodbye and looked around. The rest of Michelle's friends had left. She was alone.

"Better get used to it," she said softly.

Empty nest syndrome, wasn't that what they called it? Slowly she began to smile, wanting to do the Snoopy Dance of Joy. Empty nest was exactly what it was called and she was thrilled.

For the first time in nineteen years, she was free. She could go where she pleased and do what she wanted. She could pig out on chocolate without worrying if she was setting a good example. Or sleep late and forget about being responsible and industrious.

She could travel, time permitting. Explore the Yucatan Peninsula and old ruins. Cruise the Alaskan waterways and see an iceberg being calved. Take a trip down the Mississippi or even fly to Paris.

"Yippee for empty nests," she said softly, turning to enter the large casino which comprised much of the ground floor of the hotel where the wedding had taken place and where she had a room.

Michelle and Charlie had elected to spend their honeymoon on a trip through the gold rush country, but Ashley was spending her vacation right here at Lake Tahoe, where Stateline, Nevada, had casinos and extravagant shows and all the amenities of a world-class resort including gorgeous Lake Tahoe.

Too bad she'd never learned to ski. It seemed as if half the occupants of the hotel were skiers, looking healthy and vibrant as they walked through in their colorful clothes.

Maybe something else she could try. She was thirty-eight years old, and felt as giddy as a schoolgirl. She was going to spread her own wings at last and she could hardly wait.

But not today. It was early afternoon—she planned to spend the rest of the day at the hotel spa. First a massage, then a facial and a hair cut. She'd lap up the luxury before returning to the mundane aspects of her own life.

Hurrying through the casino floor on her way to the elevators, Ashley glanced at the people crowding the expanse. Slot machines sounded to her left. To the right were huge craps tables surrounded by excited players, less crowded tables for blackjack, and discretely tucked in the back a roped off area for the really high rollers.

She watched as one elderly lady pulled the handle on the slot machine with such an avid look of anticipation, Ashley could almost feel her excitement.

Ashley didn't gamble. She'd come by her money too hard to waste it when everyone knew the house always wins.

She bumped into someone. To her dismay, a bucket of coins flew from his hand and spilled onto the carpet. Nickels rolled everywhere.

"Oh, no, I'm so sorry," she said, scrambling to pick up as many of the coins as she could.

She barely glanced at the man, intent on recovering his money before other people realized what had happened and tried to scoop up some for their own use.

"No problem," a lazy drawl sounded above her.

He stooped down beside her and held out the bucket for the coins in her hands. She dumped them in and scooped up some more.

"I'm not usually that clumsy," she said, dropping in more coins into the plastic container.

He also skimmed a handful from the carpet. Several other players stopped to help.

"That looks about right," he said a moment later and stood.

She saw his hand and took it for assistance rising.

Then she looked at him and almost caught her breath.

Wow, she thought, glad to know her hormones hadn't permanently atrophied over the last nineteen years. She could definitely recognize a hunk when she saw one. And respond. Her heart skipped a beat then settled merrily down into double time. She could feel the flush flash through her and knew she had to take a breath. But holding it seemed easier to do.

"You look like you're on your way somewhere," he said, slowly releasing her hand. "All dressed up."

The majority of the people in the casino were wearing ski togs or casual clothes. His own dark jeans and white shirt, opened at the throat, looked superbly casual. Of course, Ashley thought wildly, everything about him looked superb.

"I just came from a wedding," she said.

He quickly glanced at her left hand, then met her eyes and smiled. "Not your own, I see."

"No, my daughter's."

Surprise flickered in his eyes. "You don't look old enough to have a marriageable daughter."

Was he flirting with her? she wondered, struck by the notion.

It'd been decades since she'd flirted with anyone. Did she remember how?

"I was a child bride," she said with a teasing smile.

"From Kentucky." He nodded.

"Kentucky?" Where had that come from?

"Obviously you married at age twelve and I hear hillbillies do that sometimes," he said.

She laughed.

He was flirting. And it felt wonderful.

"Well, I can't admit to my age, now, can I? But my daughter is very young to be getting married."

"I knew it, another twelve year old," he teased.

"No. She's nineteen."

He shifted the bucket of coins, stepped back and reached for her hand, pulling her out of the center of the aisle where they were blocking the way.

Ashley felt the reaction of his touch to her toes. She hadn't expected that.

His thumb brushed over her ring less fingers and then he slowly let go.

"Any other kids?" he asked.

"No, just the one."

"And no husband."

It was a statement. An obvious one given she wore no rings.

"And no husband."

"Are you free for dinner?"

What? He was asking her out? They hadn't even introduced themselves.

"It's the least you could do for spilling my winnings."

She glanced at the bucket, it was about half full of nickels.

"You're one of the high rollers, aren't you?" she asked with a laugh.

"Well blast it, you caught me out. But I promise, I can spend more than this on dinner."

She was tempted. Normally she wouldn't dream of letting herself be picked up.

Yet, hadn't she just promised herself she would celebrate being on her own without the respectability and duties of a mother?

Still, she had some sense of self-preservation.

"I don't know you," she said slowly.

"That'll be the fun of dinner, we can discover who each other is. I don't know you, either, but I'm willing to take a chance. It's just dinner. Tell you what, come with me while I turn these in and then try my luck on the dime machines. We'll talk and by dinner time you'll know all about me."

"Sorry, I'm on my way to the spa."

Enticing though his offer was, the lure of the spa held sway.

"Ah, a woman who enjoys sybaritic pleasures. A hot oil massage, right?"

It sounded intimate coming from him.

She nodded. If he suggested he could give her a better one, she'd turn and leave in a heartbeat.

"Relaxing, which is probably what the mother of the bride needs. I'll meet you here at seven. Don't be late."

"I didn't say I'd have dinner with you."

"Have other plans?"

Ashley shook her head before she thought. "But that—"

He placed a finger across her lips, pressing slightly.

"No excuses. Meet me here at seven. We'll eat at one of the hotel's restaurants and you can go back up to your room when we finish. Safe and sound. See you then."

He turned and headed for the cashier booth.

Ashley remained in place after he left. Vanished almost. One moment his finger had her frozen in place by the tingling sensations that coursed through her, the next, he'd melted away between the rows of slots heading for the cashier booth. She watched him for a moment, he was taller that most of the people in the casino. But when he turned a corner formed by the bank of slots machines, he was lost from sight.

Shaking her head as if to clear her brain, she continued to the elevators, watching carefully lest she bump into someone else.

She still didn't know his name. How could she have dinner with a total stranger?

How could she not, given how he looked and the reaction she felt?

For the first time in ages, Ashley felt young and full of anticipation. He'd seemed interested in her. Maybe having dinner would be fun. At least it would be daring. Live a little.

Nick Carstairs walked away without looking back, much as he was tempted. Who was she? Cute as could be, and bemused by the activity in the casino, unless he missed his guess. She obviously wasn't used to the gambling scene. Which only spoke well of her to him.

He rarely indulged himself. And then only to while away the time. His cohort, Dex, was skiing. Nick had time on his hands and didn't mind wasting a few dollars on mindless entertainment. But not at a fast clip hence the nickel and dime machines.

He handed his bucket to the change woman and waited while the coin machine calculated how many nickels he had.

She hadn't looked old enough to be a mother of a bride, he thought as he waited. Did it matter? He'd come to Tahoe to relax after the last trip and get in some serious skiing. Yesterday he and Dex burned up the slopes. Today he'd stayed inside to catch up on some work via the Internet. He'd been gone from the office more than two weeks and it'd be another few days before he returned. Couldn't let too much work pile up.

Would she join him for dinner? She'd said she was unattached, but that didn't mean she wasn't seeing someone or had a significant other in the wings.

He caught himself when he turned around, trying to see over the crowd. She was just a woman he'd met. Nothing special. So what if her dark blue eyes made him think of the Aegean sea after a storm, or her peaches and cream complexion reminded him of an Irish colleen. Her dress had been flowing, enveloping a figure he could dream about. He liked her laugh, her sparkling eyes. Everything.

He reached for the bills the cashier handed him and stepped aside, thrusting them into his pocket. An evening shared with a pretty woman sure beat listening to Dex talk about how good the ski runs were today.

He didn't need an update, he'd be out on them himself again tomorrow.

Did she ski?

Did a mother with a kid indulge in sports like that?

He'd never dated a mother before. He didn't interact well with kids and he definitely wasn't interested in being tied down by some woman who wanted a picket fence and a dog.

Not that he'd class her in that role–especially now that her child was grown and gone. It had to make her older than she looked, anyone could do the math, and their joking aside, he didn't believe she married at age twelve.

Not that age mattered. He'd enjoy the evening, no ties implied. It was only dinner.

He headed for the dime slots. Another few hours of mindless entertainment. Then he'd see if his mysterious lady would show.

As the afternoon continued, Ashley forgot her worry about Michelle and Charlie, all she could think about was the stranger in the casino. He'd been so good looking, tall, with dark hair a shade longer than the accountants she worked with wore theirs. His body was trim and fit, with a hint of muscles she wasn't used to. He seemed relaxed, yet there was a certain air of authority surrounding him.

And he sure had more than his share of sex appeal. That alone put him way out of her league. She'd rarely dated over the years. Her flirting skills were nonexistent. And she still harbored the uncertainty around men that had marked her when Darrell had taken off after Michelle's birth. They'd been high school sweethearts, certain they were destined to be together forever even over the objections of their parents.

Instead, it had been a case where her parents had known

best. They'd been furious with her and told her she'd made her bed, she was on her own. That had been before Michelle. Even her birth had not softened their stance. Consequently they'd missed out on all her childhood.

Five years ago, Ashley had learned they moved to a retirement community in Arizona. She hadn't had any contact with them in almost twenty years. Loving her daughter as she did, she didn't understand her parents' position. She'd do anything for Michelle, even if she made a mistake along the way.

Wasn't that what families were for, to support each other when hard times came? To share in the good times and love each other no matter what?

Gradually Ashley gave into the pleasurable sensations of the massage. The darkened room and soft music conspired to relax. The warm oil and soothing strokes of the masseuse were heavenly. She enjoyed the sybaritic delights. If she could have afforded it, she'd do this all the time. What would her mysterious man say to that?

By the time six-thirty rolled around, Ashley was in a state. She didn't know whether to go to dinner with a stranger or not. How safe was that?

On the other hand, if they ate in the hotel, how dangerous could it be? She wouldn't get in a car with someone she didn't know. She wouldn't go anywhere she didn't know. They'd have dinner, chat a while, and that would be that.

It beat staying in her room and ordering room service.

Especially after getting a complete make over after her massage.

She lifted the flirty sea-green dress from the bed. It'd be a shame to waste it.

For the first time in longer than she could remember, she felt like someone else. Someone full of life and anticipation. She could wear this nothing of a dress, the super high heels she bought, and flirt like crazy. Then come back safely to her room and dream about a fabulous evening like none she'd ever had.

She'd do it.

At seven o'clock she stepped from the elevator, feeling as exposed as if she were wearing a bikini. The sales woman at the boutique had assured her she looked terrific in the dress, but it clung like a second skin and didn't even reach her knees. The new, shorter hair felt as if she'd been scalped. She suspected the sultry look she'd tried for with the new makeup probably looked silly.

Before she could dash back into the elevator, however, he appeared looking as sexy as she remembered. Now he wore a dark suit, pristine-white shirt and dark tie. His eyes captured hers as he sauntered across the expanse, letting her know by his quick glance, that encompassed everything from the new hair style to the sexy heels, that he liked what he saw.

"Nicholas Carstairs," he said, holding out his hand.

"Ashley Bennett," she replied, taking his hand. Instead of shaking it, he drew her closer, tucking her hand in the crook of his elbow when he turned. He headed toward the bank of elevators that serviced the rooftop restaurant.

"I made reservations at the Starlight Room," he said. "Dinner and dancing, sound all right?"

"It sounds perfect."

All her worries fled. He wasn't trying to whisk her away somewhere. They'd stay right in the hotel and if things got awkward, she could walk back to her room.

But if the evening went well, she'd have a wonderful start on her new life.

"So tell me all about Ashley Bennett," Nick invited when they were seated beside one of the floor-to-ceiling windows overlooking the lake. It was pitch dark outside, with only the lights from town and scattered homes on the shore offering any break to the Stygian night. A cloud cover had drifted in, blotting out the stars. The windows reflected the soft lights of the restaurant.

A combo playing nearby provided excellent background music and an opportunity to dance.

Ashley looked at him, wondering what about her boring life would appeal to such a fascinating man. A look at his expensive clothes convinced her he'd know nothing about struggling to earn a living, working her way through college while raising a child.

A single man in his early thirties would know nothing about the turmoil at home when said child was a teen and angry she never met her father. Or the difficulties a woman had competing with the old boys network at work. Her life now suited her, but to tell someone else how she spent it sounded boring.

What she wanted was to have Nick consider her exciting and daring. A woman of the world, totally at ease with going out to dinner with a stranger. She wanted to forget she was a mom and have him see her as a woman of mystery. Someone he'd be glad he'd coerced into having dinner with him.

"The brief version?" she asked, stalling as she frantically tried to come up with something exciting.

"We've got all evening, why be brief?"

She leaned closer.

"All right, but you have to be discreet."

He raised an eyebrow. "How discreet?"

"I don't want my cover blown."

Amusement danced in his eyes. "You have my promise."

"I am a kind of detective, ferreting out facts people often want secreted down to the tiniest detail. Depending on the consequence, I expose them. Making them come clean on all fronts."

He looked intrigued. Ashley sat back, satisfied. She wasn't just some boring accountant who would make his eyes glaze over with talk of debits and credits. Could she expand her mysterious occupation through dinner? She'd never tried it before, but the challenge was proving to be fun.

The real key would be to tell only the truth, while giving a different impression.

"That's the short version, I suspect," he said.

She nodded. "So tell me about you."

"Maybe I'm one of the people who assists those who want to guard their information," he said, his eyes holding hers.

"What?"

"Security. Boring, I know, but there it is. My company designs and implements security systems for businesses, from basic burglar alarms, to sophisticated fire walls in mainframe computers. I'm in the computer division."

"You work with computers?"

She couldn't believe it. He looked tan, fit, athletic. How could he be stuck behind a computer all day?

"Among other aspects of the firm. Actually I'm one of the

partners. Computers are my specialty. Disappointed?"

Oh, no. He thought she was some super detective with a glamorous life and his would disappoint her. That's why she shouldn't tell tall tales.

"Not at all. I find computers fascinating. And frustrating if they don't work the way they were supposed to."

She was never able to troubleshoot problems herself, she always had to call the tech in.

"Do you work here at Lake Tahoe?" she asked.

"No. Headquarters are in San Francisco. But I travel a lot. I'm here on a break. Just got back from London."

"London?"

Her eyes widened.

"Ever been there?"

She shook her head.

"Your work is local, then?" he asked.

"San Francisco."

"Ah."

"What were you doing in London?"

She tucked away the knowledge he was also from San Francisco. Would they ever run into each other once they returned home? Would he ask her out again?

"Helping a firm set up sophisticated fire walls so hackers don't get in. Before that I was in Brussels working on some of the mainframes for the EU."

"And before that?"

She was fascinated. Imagine having a job that took him all over the world. That's what she wanted. A chance to travel and see other cultures, visit historic sites, learn to eat Italian food properly in Italy or see a bullfight in Spain.

"Hong Kong. Crowded as all get out, but exciting."

Ashley could only stare at him. He spoke about traveling as casually as she talked about going to the supermarket.

"You've been all over the world?"

He nodded.

The waiter temporarily halted their conversation as he served dinner, asking if they needed anything else. Once he departed, Ashley looked at Nick.

"I'd love to travel. In fact, I was just thinking earlier with Michelle married, I'm free for the first time in years. No ties to keep me home. I can travel whenever I want. Splurge and indulge my desires."

"Are those the only desires you wish to indulge?" he asked, softly.

Heat washed through her at the look in his eyes. She dropped her gaze to her meal and didn't answer. But a mental picture of Nick and her locked in a heated embrace immediately came to mind. Thank goodness he couldn't read her thoughts.

"Hey, buddy. I wondered where you disappeared to."

A tall man with shaggy blond hair stopped by the table, obviously addressing Nick, but with his eyes on Ashley.

"I was available for dinner, but you didn't invite me," he said.

"As you can see, I had other plans," Nick said.

"And you're not sharing?"

"No."

Ashley glanced at Nick who was looking at her with amusement. He inclined his head slightly.

"I might make an introduction if you leave immediately," he said to his friend.

"Or I could join you," he suggested, making no move to pull out one of the empty chairs at the table.

"Ashley, this obnoxious guy is a fellow partner at Aste Technologies. Dexter Braddox. Dex, Ashley Bennett. And no, you can't join us."

"We came up for the skiing and the first thing you do is dump me for work and now I find you with the prettiest woman in the place. Does that seem fair?" Dex asked.

Ashley smiled at the compliment, knowing they were kidding each other, but feeling like the center of attention between two very good-looking, successful males. She'd never been in such a situation before.

Dex chatted for another minute, then left. Ashley looked at Nick.

"Should you have invited him to join us?"

"No. I definitely didn't want him horning in on our evening. Let him find his own woman."

So Nick considered her his woman at least for the evening.

She smiled at the sheer delight she felt and resumed eating.

They discussed the food, the ambiance of the restaurant, and the activities the area held. Then Nick said, "Since we both live in the city, maybe I know where you work. Or is that top secret? Do you live near your office? Do you even have offices?"

"I live near Fort Mason and it's an easy bus ride to work on Montgomery Street where the office is located. Sometimes

I walk on really nice summer days. It's good exercise."

"We're practically neighbors, then. I have a place in the Marina district."

She nodded, knowing they might physically be not too distant, but the small apartments near Fort Mason were nothing compared to the lavish homes in the ritzy Marina district. A view of the water seemed to be required of those places. Her view was of the city buses that traveled the street.

"Who watches your place when you're gone?" she asked.

She was finished eating. Would he want to extend the evening or suggest they leave?

"My mail is sent to the office. My secretary deals with most of it. No plants, no pets, nothing that requires a lot of attention," he said.

Glancing at the dance floor, he noted several couples were dancing.

"Care to dance?" he asked, glancing at her empty plate.

Ashley had been hoping for some dessert, she'd seen a tray of fancy chocolate concoctions when they'd first entered the restaurant.

But dancing sounded almost as decadent. Not that she was a good dancer. She hadn't a lot of practice, but how hard could swaying to a slow tempo be?

She was tempted beyond resistance to be held in his arms. She'd noticed the glances from other women while they ate. Nick was the best looking man in the place and Ashley felt a wave of gratitude he seemed intent on her.

He escorted her to the small dance floor and swept her into his arms. The music was seductive. Or being held by such a sexy man was. Whatever, Ashley felt like she was a princess.

They moved together as if they'd been dance partners for years. She rested her forehead against his lower jaw, relishing the touch of skin against skin. His arm encircled her, his hand splayed over the small of her back. The slightest pressure guided her. His other hand, large and strong, held hers gently. It made her feel safe.

She'd always been the strong one in their family of two. It felt odd to feel sheltered. Odd, but nice.

"When do you return to San Francisco?" he asked.

"Not for a few days. I'm on vacation."

"Spend them with me."

2

Ashley pulled back a little so she could see his face. "Spend my vacation with you? Here at the hotel?"

"I'm staying here, so are you. We could spend our time together. You can tell me more about your job. Or where you'd travel if you had no limits. Do you ski? We could go skiing. Or if you'd rather gamble, we could do that."

"I'm afraid I don't gamble, and I don't ski. I planned to walk along the lake, catch up on some reading, maybe indulge myself at the spa again."

"Change your plans," he suggested.

Ashley didn't hesitate beyond a split second. Wasn't she yearning for adventure? Wanting something different from the last two decades? What better than to share an exciting vacation with an interesting man? No one knew her at Lake Tahoe. No one had expectations about how she should behave. No one could censure her for taking a chance.

Throwing caution to the wind and feeling very adventuresome, she nodded.

"I'd love that. You can tell me all about where you've been, to help me decide where I should go first. And I'll tell you what I can about my own job."

As long as she could figure out a way to make it sound glamorous, she could keep him intrigued. A mysterious woman to share his vacation with. What fun it was to be responsible solely for herself at long last.

An empty nest was a wondrous thing.

Nick settled her against him, relishing the feel of her feminine body against his. She fascinated him. She wasn't pestering him to reveal his intimate most secrets. She wasn't trying to impress him with all her fantastic accomplishments or all the compliments she received from other men. Consequently he didn't feel the need to try to impress or put the make on her. He was attracted to her, that was a given. She was beautiful, and fun to be with, unlike the women he'd been seeing most recently, always wanting more of his time, attention, money.

She seemed content with his idea of spending their vacation together. He'd relax and enjoy his time away from work or as much as he could allow. There'd still be time in the early mornings to catch up on things via the Internet.

For a moment cynicism rose. Was she too good to be true? She seemed eager to embrace the exact life he enjoyed. Was it a ploy or was she genuinely excited about traveling?

If so, maybe she could go with him on a trip or two. Visiting some of his favorite spots took on a new meaning when he thought about showing them to Ashley. She'd be enchanted with Paris. Fascinated by Rome and Athens. Probably amazed by the bustle and energy of crowded Hong Kong. He could envision her eyes lighting up in delight, the curve of her lips when she smiled.

Suddenly he wondered what she'd look like in bed—a combination of all the above?

Too soon the combo took a break.

"It's getting late," Ashley said as they returned to their table. "If we're going to be up early tomorrow, I'd better get some sleep."

"Are we getting up early?"

For a moment he almost suggested they finish the evening in his room. But something held him back. Ashley wasn't like the women he generally dated. She was special. He wasn't going to risk ruining what they had together by rushing things. There were several days ahead of them. Their coming together would be all the sweeter for waiting.

"I don't want to waste a minute of vacation," she said. "Besides, who knows how long the weather will hold. It could snow again any day."

He paid the check and escorted her to the elevator. They rode down, changed at the lobby and took one of the other elevators to the rooms. She told him which floor she was on. When he walked her to her door he almost invited himself in. But he resisted the impulse. He'd wait. Not easily, but he wasn't some randy young teenager. He'd acquired some polish over the last decade or so.

"I'll meet you for breakfast at eight," he suggested.

"Fine. By the elevator?"

He nodded. Raising his hand, he toyed with a short lock of her soft honey-brown hair. She'd had it cut between the first time he'd seen her and dinner. The new style suited her. Had it been highlighted? Or were the strands of gold mixed in natural? Whatever, the style made her look more sophisticated than he suspected she really was. Studying her, he was struck again by how much he was attracted her.

He leaned in and kissed her gently. Her lips were soft and

warm. She responded with an enthusiasm which surprised him. Maybe he was wrong about waiting.

Then she stepped back, fumbled with the card and opened her door.

"Thanks again for tonight."

She shut the door in his face.

Nick rocked back on his heels and looked up at the ceiling, drawing in a deep breath. Maybe he'd miscalculated. Maybe she'd have been more receptive than he'd thought.

It wasn't even midnight, but he might as well get to bed. He didn't want to be a second late for breakfast.

"Wow. Oh, wow," Ashley said softly, leaning against the door.

He'd kissed her.

She hadn't been kissed since that sloppy attempt by Jack Renner seven years ago. She couldn't call that a kiss, more like a wet puppy's salutation.

Nick Carstairs, on the other hand, could corner the market on kisses. She felt herself tingle all over and her smile wouldn't stop. Pushing away from the door, she danced around the room, imagining Nick's arms around her. She'd *loved* their evening together.

A week of his company. She couldn't believe it. Would they get bored? Or find they wanted more than a week? They both lived in San Francisco. Maybe he'd ask her out when they returned home.

She got ready for bed, thinking of all the possibilities, feeling almost giddy with happiness. The worry about Michelle and Charlie was long forgotten.

The next day was one of the best Ashley ever spent. At

breakfast Nick tried to talk her into skiing. But she refused, choosing instead to walk along the water's edge. She suggested he go with his friend and meet her later. She'd be disappointed, but she could handle that. She didn't relish making a fool of herself the first day trying to learn to ski with an expert watching.

To her gratification, Nick dismissed her suggestion and insisted he'd rather spend the day with her.

"I've been skiing for years. And have had two good days here already. The mountains will always be here. Let's get some coffee to keep us warm and tackle that walk."

The snow had melted enough to reveal the sandy beach. They battled the wind that swept across the lake, but with the sunshine and warm jackets, the day felt exhilarating.

Nick bought coffee for them to take, and when they found a sheltered spot, complete with bench, they sat down to sip the warm beverage. The wavelets driven by the wind breaking against the shore rendered a soft melodious background. The water sparkled in the sunshine. The snow on the surrounding peaks gleamed like thousands of diamonds with the tall green conifers and deep blue sky startling contrasts.

Ashley drank in the beauty as she tried to imprint every aspect of the day on her memory. Especially the man beside her.

"Tell me about London," Ashley invited, looking at him over the edge of her cup as she took another welcomed sip.

"If we take turns."

"You know all about San Francisco," she said.

"But not all about you. I want every speck of information I can get," Nick said.

Flattered, she nodded, hugging the compliment to herself. Don't get carried away, she admonished. He's on vacation and making the most of it.

"Okay, but you start with London," she said, yearning to hear about his travels, his work, every scrap of information he'd give. Did he really feel the same about her?

"Tenacious," he commented, then began to describe the events of his last trip.

When he'd finished, she frowned.

"If I'd been there, I'd have visited the museums, walked in Piccadilly Circus, and definitely done some shopping. You went to work and back to the hotel. Boring."

"It's my fourth visit. Besides, winter in London doesn't exactly lend itself to strolling around. To say the least, it's cold there. And I had a job to do."

She watched the way his eyes seemed to delve into her. He looked at her a lot, as if he liked what he saw. She felt flustered.

What had they been talking about? Oh, the weather. Somehow in her fantasies about travel, it had always been perpetual summer.

"Tell me how you cope with the language barrier when you travel to other countries. Especially in dealing with computer work," she asked, wishing he'd talk all day.

She liked his voice, the expressions on his face, the way his eyes looked at her, into her. She had never felt another's attention so completely.

"When in countries where I don't speak the language, I

hire an interpreter. When I was in Hong Kong last time I had an old guy who loved to wax poetic about the glory days of the Chinese empire which ended long before he was born."

He continued telling her some of the funny things his guide had said.

He had a way with words that painted pictures in her mind of the sights he'd seen. She felt as if she'd been to London and Hong Kong, though she sure would have done more sightseeing if she visited those locations. Would he want to do more in his free time if he had someone to share the adventure with?

By the time they finished their coffee, they were ready to walk again. It was too cold to sit for long.

"Now I want to hear about you and your exciting job," Nick said, taking her hand. Ashley glanced at their linked hands, then laughed in sheer joy.

"I'm so sorry to disappoint you, Nick, but it's not so exciting."

She regretted her attempts to make herself more than she was. Would he be disgusted at her ploy?

"Ferreting out hidden facts? Detection work, right?"

"Some of it. Actually I'm an accountant. I audit books for companies and work on taxes. Not very exciting, I'm afraid. But I like it."

"You sound defensive. I assume you like your work or you'd do something else," he said easily.

At least he wasn't annoyed she'd tried to make it sound more glamorous than it was. She nodded, never having thought about it that way. She liked dealing with numbers. They were logical and predictable. They never let her down like people did. They were safe.

The day flew by as they explored their section of the shoreline. Pleasure boats were tied at a marina, covered and unused in winter. Many of the large homes that fronted the lake were also closed, though here and there smoke came from chimneys of those occupied. They ventured onto Main Street, wandering around the shops selling crafts and memorabilia.

They ate lunch at an outdoor café, with heaters to keep the patrons warm. In the best of the German tradition, they'd eaten bratwurst and sauerkraut. Surrounding them were skiers taking a lunch break and an occasional family with children running around and playing in the snow near the deck.

"I'll meet you here at seven," Nick said when they reached the elevator bank in the hotel in the late afternoon. "Do you want to eat at the Starlight room again or try another place?" he asked.

"Surprise me," she said, taking her shopping bags from his fingers, her own brushing his at the transfer.

He'd touched her often during the day, holding her hand while they walked along the beach, placing his hands on her shoulders when they had to go single file in some of the crowded shops. She should be getting used to his touch, but she felt flustered every time.

"Till seven, then," he said, leaning over to brush his lips against hers.

It didn't bother him they were in the busy lobby of a major hotel, with dozens of people milling around and slot machines sounding. It was just a brief touch, yet Ashley felt it to her toes.

Stunned, she stepped into the elevator and watched the doors close between them. She needed to watch herself–he was way out of her league. This was only a vacation, a slice of time out of the ordinary.

But as she remembered every moment of the day, she fantasized about sharing more than a vacation with him. That's what being married should have been like. What building a life together could have been.

She'd missed out on so much when Darrell left. She should have done something about it years ago but she'd put relationships on hold for Michelle's sake.

Or was it about meeting a special man who had her fantasizing about such things?

She quickly dumped the packages on her bed in her room and then headed back down to the lobby shops in search of another dress. The only dresses she had were her mother-of-the-bride dress and the new one she'd bought yesterday. The rest of her wardrobe consisted of the warm pants and thick tops which were all she had anticipated needing for her vacation.

Nick had seen yesterday's purchase, she wanted something new for tonight.

She chose a subdued dress in dark hunter-green and splurged on a gold chain necklace. The two went together perfectly. Dashing back up to her room, she showered, dressed and got ready for the evening. Excitement built as she impatiently waited for seven o'clock. She missed him and it had only been two hours since she'd seen him.

She couldn't believe how easily the two of them had meshed. Conversation never lagged, yet there were still worlds to share. Dancing, holding hands, kisses–she couldn't wait.

Ashley awoke Wednesday morning with a feeling of impeding doom. Today was her last day of vacation. She had to head for home this afternoon, and start back at the office tomorrow.

She didn't want to end their idyllic time.

Lying back she snuggled beneath the covers, remembering every moment she and Nick had spent over the last few days. Every single one had been special.

She was afraid she was falling in love. How crazy was that? He was younger than she by several years, though neither had made mention of the fact. He traveled the world while she had never been much farther from California than Nevada.

And he was so sexy it made her teeth ache. His casual touch set her heart racing. His kisses each night had grown more ardent. Last night she thought for sure he'd push for more than a few hot kisses. But he remained a gentlemen every time.

Or maybe he didn't feel as she did. Perhaps it was no hardship to leave her at her door and saunter away in that sexy male walk of his. It could be she was merely someone to spend his vacation with beside Dexter. Somehow being a notch above his shaggy-haired friend wasn't the best comparison.

Speculation was futile. She'd know soon enough. He hadn't asked her for her phone number. Maybe this was just a vacation fling, a special time that would fade into a pleasant memory once she returned to home.

She hoped not.

Once dressed, she began to pack. She'd check out by eleven, but could stay until late afternoon and still make it home before bedtime. Since it was the middle of the week, the traffic on the interstate wouldn't be heavy.

Maybe Nick would ask to ride down with her. Had he brought a car or come with Dex? It was odd she knew about his most recent trip to London, but didn't have that current fact.

Nick stood waiting at the elevators when she stepped into the lobby. He'd never not been there, even yesterday when she'd come down five minutes early. That had to be a good sign, didn't it?

His smile set her pulses pounding again. She took a deep breath, hoping he'd ask to see her again. What if today was the last time they were together?

"I thought we'd walk over to the pancake house, splurge on a big breakfast we'll then have to spend the day walking off," he said, reaching out for her hand.

"Sounds great."

She laced her fingers through his, a standard practice. Everything they had done together had been special because he'd been a part of it.

"Sure you don't want to try skiing?" he asked.

It might be her last chance. They'd done everything else the area had to offer why not? She'd still be clumsy and he was probably an expert. But it was something he liked. She could end up loving it.

"Okay, I'll give it a try."

He squeezed her hand in approval as they headed for the pancake house.

"You'll love it. And I'm an expert teacher."

No sooner had their breakfasts been served than his cell phone rang.

Ashley couldn't help hearing his side of the conversation

and her heart dropped. There would be no skiing today. He was being called to some emergency.

"Sorry, Ashley, I have to go," Nick said clicking off the phone a few minutes later.

"An emergency, I got that from your side of the conversation," she said evenly, though she wanted to rail against fate. "Do you have to leave immediately?"

"I can finish breakfast. Let me call the hotel and see if I can catch Dex before he hits the slopes. I need him to get me to Reno. They've already booked me on a flight from there."

Ashley could scarcely eat her pecan pancakes. Usually her favorite, the food stuck in her throat every time she tried to swallow.

Only a few more minutes before he left. The refrain echoed in her mind.

As soon as she finished, they hurried back to the hotel. She could already feel the distance growing between them. He was focused on the tasks ahead. While not quite forgotten, he was still holding her hand, his attention no longer concentrated on her.

She'd known they'd say goodbye today. She had expected it to be later. After he'd asked for her home phone number.

Dex met them in the lobby.

"They've confirmed your space on the 12:15 flight to Denver. You change there for Boston, and then have a red-eye to Amsterdam. You have your passport with you, right?"

Nick nodded. "And laptop. I could use some other clothes, but I'll pick something up in Amsterdam. I'll go up and pack. Can you take my suitcase back with you?"

"Sure enough." Dex looked at his watch. "We need to get going to make that flight from Reno."

"Give us a minute, will you?" Nick asked.

He drew Ashley to the elevators and punched the button.

"You don't need to walk me to my room, Nick. I know time is short and you still need to pack. We can say goodbye here. Thanks for such a special vacation."

She kept her voice level, steady. She refused to burst into tears as she wanted. They'd never talked about the future, nor made any promises. He was free to go where he had to, as was she.

He turned her toward him, resting his hands on her shoulders.

"You're one special lady, Ashley. Next time I take a vacation, I want you to share it with me."

He kissed her again as if they were the only two people in the world and not a couple in the midst of a bustling lobby.

The elevator arrived.

"Go pack and catch your flight. Do some sightseeing in Amsterdam for me," she said when he looked at the opened door.

She gently pushed him away and watched the doors close behind him.

Her vacation was over.

Blast it all, Nick thought as he rode to his room. He couldn't believe the timing. Why did the program have to fail at this point? Now it was up to him to repair the damage, not only to the computer, but also to the good will of the company.

He played hard, but he worked hard, too. He and Dex and Tony had started the company seven years ago. It had expanded beyond their wildest dreams back then. And all of them, and the other employees they'd hired over the years, wanted to keep it on top. He was a major player in keeping them in the forefront. But today he wished someone else could have been sent to Amsterdam.

He wanted to stay with Ashley.

Frowning, he entered his room and began to pack. Where had that thought come from? He loved traveling. He'd decided long ago when living with Uncle Henry that given the chance, he'd travel the world and never look back.

He'd done just that. And relished every assignment. Going off into the unknown sure beat a routine nine-to-five job that would have bored him in no time.

He never wanted to end up bitter and complaining as Uncle Henry had been. Tied down, unhappy in his work, in his life, the old man had never hidden his resentment at the unfairness of his life.

Nick had left Henry's place at eighteen to work his way through college. He'd known an education was the key to getting out of the rat race his uncle complained about. And he had. He'd visited all the major cities of the world. Vacationed in some of the most exotic and exciting locales known to man.

But this time the adrenaline rush was missing. He'd have rather stayed with Ashley.

She was the perfect companion. Each day had been special. His only regret was he hadn't pushed harder to spend those nights together as well.

Lively, fun, and enchanted by mundane things, she gave a new view to everything. The days had flown by. Now he had to leave before he was ready. A first. Usually he was raring to go to a new city, face new challenges.

They'd made no promises.

Suddenly he realized he hadn't even gotten her phone number. What if she didn't have a land line? How would he ever find her cell number? He lunged for the room phone and punched in her room number. The phone rang and rang, finally clicking over to voice mail. Wouldn't do any good to leave a message, he wouldn't be here for her to call back.

Maybe she'd stayed downstairs to talk to Dex. If she had, he could ask her then.

If not, he'd get Dex to find out when he returned from dropping him at the airport. It was the best he could do. He threw a few things in the carry all, including his laptop. The rest went into the suitcase for Dex. He'd have to buy some clothes in Amsterdam. At least they didn't expect computer experts to dress up in suits and ties.

Forty-five minutes later Dex dropped him at the curb at Reno-Tahoe Airport.

"Don't forget, get her phone number. Tell her I'll call her as soon as I get back to San Francisco," Nick said.

"Hey, old buddy, you've only repeated yourself a dozen times on the ride here. I couldn't possibly forget. I'll have the number for you today. Look at your e-mail when you get to Amsterdam. If I didn't know you better, I'd think you've fallen for the pretty lady," Dex said.

He waved and drove off.

Nick stared after him. Fallen for Ashley? No, but he'd like to see her again.

Ashley saw no reason to stay once Nick had gone. She finished packing, checked out early and headed for home. There were wedding presents in the trunk of her car Michelle had asked her to take back for her. The kids would be coming home later this week. She'd want to hear all about the honeymoon.

Would Michelle ask about her stay in Tahoe? And if she did, what would Ashley say? I met the most wonderful man in the world? We had a fabulous four days, then he left for Amsterdam? If Ashley had her way, it would have been the first of many days together. But Nick hadn't said a word about the future.

Better not to say anything. She'd hold the memory of their special days to her heart. But practicality reasserted itself the closer she came to San Francisco. It had been a vacation fling. He hadn't even asked for her phone number. Never even given her the classic brush-off line of *I'll call you.* Saying he wanted to spend his next vacation with her was even more vague.

Darn it, she'd loved every second spent with Nick. She'd gladly spend all her vacations with him.

And he hadn't even asked for her phone number.

By the following Friday Ashley had made some changes in her life. She wanted to plunge into sweeping changes, but found work too hectic. She'd stopped off twice at the travel agency near the office to gather packets and brochures of exotic places. She was planning to splurge on her next vacation and take one of the trips she longed for.

The frantic tax season had grabbed hold with a vengeance.

Some companies had still not closed their book for the previous year. Others had audits that required readjustments to stated expenses or capital improvements. Others were looking for creative ways to defer some of the money owed until their cash flow improved.

Any trips would have to wait until after April, but she could start planning now.

When one of the new accountants asked her out, she said yes once tax season was over. He hadn't seemed to notice her before. Had the make over at Lake Tahoe caused him to see her differently? Or was her outlook on life different these days?

Michelle came over Saturday night alone. Charlie was on duty. While happy in her new married life, she was a bit miffed things weren't going as she'd expected.

"He's still living on base at Monterey. He plans to come to the apartment when he can, but it feels as if we're still dating. I hate this limbo. We don't even know where we'll be living after his next tour. And he's reporting to San Diego in another couple of weeks. Once the ship returns to port, he can request another assignment. If he gets posted to a U.S. base next, we want to see if I can get into a nearby college," Michelle finished.

"You can always apply once you know and list the extenuating circumstances. The worse case would be wait a semester before enrolling."

Ashley didn't like that idea, but it was the best she could offer to cheer up her daughter. At least she was in school this term and wasn't flying off to a naval base on the east coast.

"What did you do after we left? Did you go to the spa like

you talked about?" Michelle asked as she began to make a salad to accompany the spaghetti Ashley was preparing.

"I did. And on the way met the most fantastic man who asked me to dinner."

"Was it fun?"

"Yes. To both."

"I like what you've done to your hair. You know, Mom, you could start dating again. I know I held you back. You should get married and have your own life now."

"You never held me back. I have a wonderful life just as it is," Ashley said quickly, trying not to think about her initial thoughts after the wedding that she was once again free to do whatever she wanted.

She loved her daughter. But she was a woman and wanted the attention of a special man. Nick. What would it be like to be married to him?

Fantastic, of that she had no doubt. They'd travel, visit exciting cities she'd only been able to dream about. Maybe she could learn some of the languages, to better fit in when they stayed in Madrid or Rome.

"But it's different now. I'm gone. I have my own apartment. Once Charlie knows where he'll be next, I'll be moving there. You'll be alone," Michelle persisted.

"I have lots of friends."

And lots of plans. But she didn't want to share them with anyone just yet. She enjoyed daydreaming about how she was going to change her life.

"I know, but it's not the same," Michelle said.

She was right about that. For four glorious days, Ashley had been part of a couple. She and Nick had been practically inseparable. She loved that. It had been so long since she'd been half a couple, it seemed completely new and different.

Of course, Nick made it memorable. She definitely planned to start dating, to seeing if there was someone out there with whom she could share her life. Doing things with another person sure beat doing it all by herself.

But not just yet. She suspected no one could measure up to Nick.

"We'll see. Right now isn't such a good time. Tax season, remember?"

Should she tell Michelle about Nick? Or the invitation from the man in her office?

"I know. But come the end of April would be a terrific time. Think about it, Mom."

The problem was, Ashley couldn't stop thinking about her and Nick. The days at Lake Tahoe seemed like some fairy-tale story. She remembered the walks along the beach, the fun they'd had just talking. She especially remembered the kisses.

As one week drifted into two and she heard nothing from him, she knew she had to let that dream go. He would have returned to San Francisco long ago. Did he even remember the time they'd spent together? Or was she only one in a long line of women he dated?

She looked up Aste Technologies in the phone book. It was headquartered on Montgomery Street, not too far from her own office. She hadn't resorted to seeking him out. He'd given her no indications he wanted to see her again.

Not that knowing that stopped her from looking closely

at every dark-haired man she passed on Montgomery Street. But she drew the line at deliberately walking by his company in the hopes of running into him.

Late Wednesday afternoon Ashley asked her secretary to order in a sandwich for her before she left for the day. She had scads more work to do and there was no one waiting at home. If she had something to eat, she'd be good to go for another few hours once the office closed.

She leaned back in her chair, resting her tense shoulders and gazing at the colorful poster she'd hung of Greece. She'd much rather be strolling along the ruins of the Parthenon than doing taxes for Herberty Construction.

This weekend, she planned to buy a few things to wear when she went to Greece. Or to take that cruise to Alaska, she thought as she looked at the other poster this one of deep blue seas and glorious glaciers.

Her desk phone rang. She picked it up, sighing as she returned to reality.

"Do you have any idea of how many Bennetts there are in San Francisco?" a familiar voice asked in her ear.

"Nick?" Her heart rate sped up.

"I forgot to get your phone number. You'd checked out by the time Dex got back to the hotel. So I've been making calls to every accounting agency in the city ever since I got off the flight home a couple of hours ago. I'm an idiot for not getting your number. I've missed you."

Ashley couldn't say a word.

It was Nick.

She'd given up all hope of hearing from him again.

"I can't believe it," she said softly. "I thought you got back ages ago."

"Nope. The problem turned out to be bigger than we thought. Then since I was already in The Netherlands, I took an assignment in Antwerp. But now I'm back and wanting to see you. Have dinner with me. I'll be there in ten minutes."

"It's only five-thirty, a bit early for dinner," she stalled.

The stack of work on her desk hadn't magically shrunk while she talked.

For the first time since she'd been hired, she didn't care.

Dinner with Nick—she couldn't refuse.

"Do you know where I work?"

"I can find it. But before that, give me your mobile number. I'm not hanging up until I get it."

Ashley gave it to him, and then ran her fingers through her hair.

"I'm not dressed for dinner."

"I don't care how you're dressed or even if you're dressed. I'll be there in ten minutes."

The line went dead.

Ashley gave a soft laugh of excitement.

Nick was back and wanted to see her. She almost danced from the office. She had no other responsibilities to get in the way. Imagine going off on such short notice. She loved this empty nest life.

She told Stacey to cancel the sandwich order, then dashed to the ladies room to repair her makeup. She wished she'd worn something besides black slacks and a primrose silk blouse. Perhaps one of her new dresses or something sexy to get his attention.

Nick said he didn't care. And she didn't dare take time to go home and change. She couldn't wait to see him.

Exactly nine minutes later she stepped out on the sidewalk in front of her building. The traffic moved as it did every day at rush hour, with stops and starts. She heard the toot of a horn and saw the low-slung sports car swerve to the curb. Nick climbed out, his eyes finding hers in an instant.

"Ashley."

"Nick."

For a moment, she couldn't speak. He looked just as gorgeous as he had in Lake Tahoe. She longed to touch him. Wished he'd kiss her. Giddy with happiness, she smiled.

"I'm so glad to see you."

Not very sophisticated, but heartfelt. She wanted to stand and take him all in. She hadn't realized exactly how much she'd missed him, exactly how much she'd been afraid she'd never hear from him again. The intervening days since they'd been together vanished. It was as if they'd seen each other yesterday.

"I brought you something from Antwerp," he said, walking around the rear of the car.

He leaned over and kissed her lightly on the lips.

"Get in before some cop gives me a ticket for illegal parking."

She slid into the soft leather interior, feeling as shy as a teenager.

"You've stopped. You're not parked."

"Think that'll hold up as a defense?" he asked, going around to climb into the driver's seat.

"Where would you like to go for dinner?" he said when they started moving.

"Wherever."

"London?" he suggested.

She laughed.

"Yes. Except I don't think we can get there before I starve to death."

No one else she knew would suggest London for dinner. Oh how she wished they could.

"I know a great Italian place in Columbus Square," he said.

"I love Italian," she said, watching as he competently merged the car into the traffic.

Dinner with Nick sure beat a takeout sandwich at her desk. Any meal with Nick beat that. For a fleeting second she considered all the work waiting, then promptly pushed the thought away. She was taking time with Nick, she hadn't seen him in too long. There was a limit to how much she wanted to give to the office.

"Tell me about your trip," she invited, wanting to know how he spent every moment. Had he missed her after all?

"The first emergency was successfully handled, from a business stand point," he replied.

"Is there another point?"

He flicked her a glance.

"I didn't used to think so, but this time I found myself wishing you'd been in Amsterdam with me. You'd love it. We could have sampled a different restaurant every night, taken an excursion boat on the river. The shopping's fabulous. I bet you'd like Antwerp even more. It's charming. Old, old buildings, monuments, fountains. Talk about walking around, you'd never come back to the hotel."

She sighed softly. "Maybe one day."

He nodded.

Before long they were seated in a small alcove at the Italian restaurant he liked, the heavenly fragrance of oregano and garlic filling the air.

"What did you do while I was gone?" Nick asked once their order had been taken.

"Worked. I had dinner one night with Michelle. Otherwise, we're coming into tax season and the workload increases. Nothing exciting like visiting The Netherlands."

She wasn't sure if she should tell him about her plans for her next vacation. Would he come with her?

"I wasn't exactly visiting I was working," he protested, the amusement in his eyes letting her know his kind of work in a foreign setting didn't compare to hers.

"So are you back for long?" she asked.

"I have to reconfirm my next assignment with the office to make sure it's still a go. But I'm home for a few days."

"When did you get back?"

Had he not been in his office yet?

He looked at his watch.

"About two and a half hours ago. I called around looking for you while at the airport. One of the guys at the office dropped my car for me at the airport. Saved time."

She couldn't believe her ears. He'd been as anxious to see her as she was to see him. Then another thought struck.

"You must be exhausted. You're still on European time."

"I'll last through dinner at least. I wanted to see you."

"We can eat fast," she offered, touched more than she wanted to admit at his words.

He looked uncomfortable, glanced around then looked back at her.

"I brought you something from Antwerp," he said.

She remembered he'd said that earlier. As if excited that she would like his present, to let her know he'd been thinking of her even when apart. She hadn't had a present from anyone but Michelle in years.

"A present?" she asked.

"Sort of." He fumbled in his pocket and pulled out a jewelers box.

Ashley stared at it, her breath caught in her throat. Most of the time that would be a ring box, but surely he hadn't bought her a ring.

When he flipped open the lid, she blinked at the sparkling diamond ring nestled in velvet.

"Will you marry me, Ashley?"

3

Ashley stared at the ring, then slowly raised her eyes to his. "Marry you?" she whispered.

"I was hoping you missed me as much as I missed you. We had a great time at Lake Tahoe. Think of the life we could have together. We're perfect for each other. Our lifestyles match. Quit your job, come with me wherever I go. I can arrange to take some extra time with most assignments so it won't be all work. I'm going to London next week, if the assignment still holds. I still need to verify that. If so, let's spend our honeymoon there."

He'd never asked a woman to marry him before. But Ashley was different. She was easy to be with, and fun at the same time, not to mention sexy.

He didn't have to worry about her wanting to start a family and buying some house in the suburbs, her daughter was already grown. He could easily support them. They could travel, maybe make London their home for a few years while he concentrated on European accounts. That would save time flying over every couple of weeks.

Ashley was in shock. She'd known him less than a week, all told. He was virtually a stranger. How could she marry a stranger?

Yet she had loved every moment they spent together.

She'd forever remember the fabulous days at Lake Tahoe. She'd also remember the indecision and worry that he wouldn't call. She loved being with him. Her fantasies all centered around Nick. She'd known she'd fallen for him.

But marriage?

Forever?

Would it be possible?

For a moment she let herself dream

What did she want? To spend her life doing the accounts for businessmen who argued every point with her or spend it jetting to the far flung corners of the world with the most exciting man she'd ever met?

Dare she take such a risk and go for it?

She was footloose and fancy free. Michelle had her own life with Charlie. Why not grab the happiness that dangled so temptingly in front of her?

As the seconds ticked by, Nick's expression grew more impassive.

"Forget it," he said, flipping shut the box. "Silly idea."

"It's not at all. You caught me by surprise, but I say yes."

She felt young and alive and daring all rolled up into one. She hadn't felt this way since ever.

He rose and pulled her to her feet, kissing her like she'd never been kissed before. Several of the other patrons of the restaurant clapped, obviously knowing something was going on.

When the waiter hurried over, Nick stepped back.

"Champagne, please, she's agreed to marry me."

Once he was seated, he reached for her hand, slipping the ring on her finger. It fit perfectly.

"I wasn't sure you'd even call," Ashley said, studying the sparkling stone in total disbelief. Had she really agreed to marry Nick?

"You must have known I'd find you again. You're too special to let go," he said, taking her fingers in his hand, caressing the backs with his thumb. "This is probably rushing things, but I want you, Ashley, and I don't want some other guy honing in on my woman."

"That sounds like a pick up line," she teased, not sure how to handle the emotions that threatened to overwhelm her.

Oh, she'd have to cancel her date with Tim, she thought briefly, staring into Nick's eyes. How could she ever have thought she'd enjoy herself with someone else?

"I have never told another woman that. Nor asked another woman to marry me. Actually I never thought I'd marry. But you and I will be perfect together. We'll make the entire world ours. We'll travel. Sometime on business, but plenty of time on our own. You can make up a list of all the sights you want to see. The world will be our backyard. There's nothing to tie us down."

"Sounds fabulous. I pick London first. No, wait, maybe Paris."

"We'll get to them all eventually."

He kissed her fingers, squeezing gently in affection.

The comment he made sank in.

"You never thought to marry, why not? You're terrific. Any woman would be delighted to share her life with you."

She looked at him, still a bit shocked she'd agreed to marry again. Her brief experience in wedded bliss hadn't been strong enough to recommend she try again.

With Nick it would be so different.

"Ah, a man will never tire of having his future wife think he's fabulous."

The champagne arrived and the waiter poured them both a glass, setting them before them with a flourish.

"To my wife-to-be," Nick said, raising his glass to her.

Wife. Ohmygosh, Ashley thought, as panic suddenly struck. She was going to be a wife again. To trust her future to this man she'd only met a few weeks ago. Had she lost her mind?

"To us," she said, touching her glass to his.

Granted, she hadn't known him for long, but she trusted Nick in a very basic way. And knowing someone for ages didn't guarantee anything, look at her and Darrell. They'd known each other for years and he had walked out without a look back. Some men were steadfast, some weren't.

"If we marry next week we can make London our honeymoon, who knows after that?" Nick said.

"You're serious about next week?" she asked. "And London?"

"Of course, weren't you? You do have a passport, don't you?"

She shook her head. Why would she have needed a passport before now, she never traveled.

"Not to worry, we'll get one through the office. They expedite things all the time with new employees. I'm sure we can get you one in time. Do you want to get married in a church or at City Hall?"

"My church, please. And I'll have to arrange some time

off from work. Good thing I have a lot of vacation time accrued."

The enormity of what she'd agreed to began to sink in. And vacation time owed or not, her boss would have a fit with her taking off during tax season. And what would everyone say—no one even knew she'd been seeing anyone.

"Quit your job, cut your ties, let's fly where the mood takes us. After London, we'll sit down and decide what you'd like to see first and then I'll see what assignments I can wrangle for those locations. With the threat of terrorist activities or global viruses, there are more and more assignments each month at the firm. We are expanding almost faster than we can train representatives."

"I'd love to see all of Europe, then work our way down under to Australia and New Zealand," she said, as giddy as a child at Christmas. Her lifelong dreams were coming true.

And she'd see them all with Nick. How fantastic was that?

Her heart raced, almost hurting with so much happiness. Whoever would have thought Ashley Bennett would one day be married again and off to see the world?

"Oh, where will we live? My apartment isn't very spacious," she said, reality inserting itself.

It was downright small. And Michelle still had a lot of her things there.

Michelle!

She'd have to tell her daughter right away. What would Michelle think about getting a stepfather at this late date?

"We'll get a place of our own. My apartment's small, too. We'll find something we both like and combine households," Nick said.

"I need to call Michelle. She'll want to meet you."

Michelle was going to be shocked. None of this sounded like the old Ashley.

He shook his head. "I never figured myself as father material. Good thing she's grown and married. Maybe we could all have dinner tomorrow night."

"I'll call her as soon as we get home."

She hoped Michelle liked Nick. What if she didn't?

No, that was the wrong attitude. How could she not like him?

Dinner arrived and Ashley spent the rest of the time quizzing Nick on where they'd go in London and how long they'd stay. She came up with a dozen things she'd need to do to get ready for a wedding in a week's time.

"I can't believe we're doing this," she said as they left the restaurant.

"Second thoughts?" he asked.

"Not one. I can hardly wait."

When he pulled into the curb at her apartment, she invited him up.

"Much as I'd love to, sweetheart, I'm bushed. I've been up more than twenty-four hours now and need to get some sleep. I'll call you tomorrow afternoon and we'll decide where to take Michelle and Charlie for dinner," he said.

His kiss belied his fatigue, despite the contortions they had to do in the small car. Ashley's entire body was pulsing with desire and delight by the time he ended the embrace. She wished he'd come up more than ever. But she could wait. Their coming together would be all the sweeter with anticipation.

As soon as she entered the apartment, she called Michelle.

"It's short notice I realize. But can you and Charlie have dinner with me tomorrow? I want you to meet someone special. His name is Nick Carstairs."

"Who is he?"

"As of this evening, he's my fiancé," Ashley said.

The silence at the other end was deafening.

"Michelle?"

Maybe she should have explained more before blurting out the news. But she wanted to shout it from the rooftops. Nick Carstairs wanted to marry her, Ashley Bennett.

"Mom, did you say fiancé?"

"I did."

"I didn't even know you were dating. When did all this happen?"

"The proposal was tonight. We're planning to be married next week. We're honeymooning in London."

Honeymooning. London. Ashley still couldn't believe the words tripped from her mouth so easily. She wished they were already married. It had only been moments since he'd left and she missed him.

"Next week? Mom, I haven't even met the guy. How can you get married so soon? And why? You don't have to, do you? I mean, you're not pregnant or anything are you?"

Michelle sounded worried.

"No, I'm not pregnant. I've had my family, you know that. Nick and I met in Lake Tahoe right after your wedding. We spent several glorious days together and realized when he got home tonight how much we missed each other."

"So you're getting married next week? Couldn't you, um, be engaged for a while?"

"You and Charlie got married with short notice."

Great, now she was comparing herself with her daughter. It was enough that she knew her own mind. She didn't need to justify her decision with anyone, not even Michelle.

Maybe there was a hint of uncertainty lurking, but she wouldn't admit it. She wanted to marry Nick, explore the world, live a little. She was only thirty-eight years old, not too old to still have fun.

"I haven't even met the guy," Michelle wailed.

"I know. Nick and I want to invite you and Charlie to dinner tomorrow night. You can meet him then."

"I can't say if Charlie can make it. He's at the base and has been working late most nights. He's been staying in Monterey rather than drive all the way back here. I'll see. But I'm definitely coming. In fact, maybe I'll come over to your place now. Is he there?"

"No, he just got in from Amsterdam. He's been up for twenty-four hours and needed rest. You can meet him tomorrow."

"Gosh, Mom, this doesn't sound a bit like you."

Ashley smiled as she ended the call. It didn't sound like the old her. But it was definitely the new.

Dinner the next evening went as well as expected. Michelle spent most of the meal questioning Nick. He didn't seem to mind and Ashley liked learning more about her future husband. Charlie hadn't made it, but Michelle said he'd try to make the wedding itself.

The week flew by. Ashley and Nick spent as much time together as they could with their respective work schedules.

His kisses left her breathless. His touch sent her senses into overdrive. But he restrained himself every night, leaving her at the door of her apartment as if afraid the temptation for more than kisses would be too strong if he came into her home. She was honored and frustrated by the respect he showed.

They would be married forever, he said. He could wait a few more days before consummating their love.

Thursday morning dawned cold and clear. The sky was a deep blue, without clouds. The breeze from the Bay was light, though chilly. The weather was perfect for a wedding.

Ashley found a cream-colored dress to wear, complete with wispy hat to give it a bridal touch.

She'd arranged for time off again from work, though her boss, Mr. Popovich, was concerned that she be able to get all her clients handled in the time remaining until the tax deadline.

She hadn't told him of her intent to quit. She wouldn't leave him in the lurch, but the plans she and Nick had made were important, too. She couldn't wait to be off to explore the world.

The ceremony went without a hitch. Dex was Nick's best man and Michelle stood up with her mother. She hadn't fully accepted the idea, but was cordial to Nick. She kept eyeing Ashley as if she was one brick short of a load. She voiced no objections to the wedding, but had constantly questioned Ashley on her certainty that it was the right move right up until last night. Seeing her mother was adamant, she gave in with good grace.

Once the formalities were taken care of, there was a small

reception. Ashley and Nick had invited a dozen or so friends each. The church hall held them all easily. Soft music played in the background. The caterer had prepared a light lunch complete with wedding cake.

At one point during the reception, she and Nick became separated. She spoke with old friends, laughed at the teasing from her coworkers about her whirlwind courtship, and kept an eye on things to make sure everyone was enjoying the event.

Already missing Nick, she spotted him in conversation with Dex and headed their way. Their backs were to her, but she didn't care. She'd just slip to his side and see how long it took him to notice her.

"I can't believe the playboy of the western world is now a married man," Dex was saying as she drew closer.

Ashley smiled. So Nick had a playboy reputation, interesting, if not surprising. Look how quickly he'd charmed her at the casino in Reno.

"Why not, Ashley's perfect for me. She's had her family, isn't yearning for a house and white picket fence. She wants to travel, and we all know my job has me on the road three weeks out of four. I tell you, Dex, she's the best thing to happen to me. We can explore every city I'm assigned, take some trips to others when we can. We'll still have a home base here in San Francisco. What's not to like about married life?"

"No kids in the picture?"

Ashley hesitated a moment.

They'd never discussed children. The only reference Nick had made was an offhand comment about how he couldn't picture himself as a father. Would he want children?

"That's the beauty of it, she's had her family. Michelle's all grown and doesn't need a stay-at-home mother. And let's face it, can you picture me as a father?" Nick asked.

"Don't let your past color your future, friend," Dex said. "You never pictured yourself as a husband, either, and yet here you are."

Past? The comment puzzled Ashley. Nick said he'd grown up under the care of an uncle. Had something happened to put him off having children?

He turned and saw her, his slow smile turning her insides mushy.

"Come here, Mrs. Carstairs, Dex was just telling me how envious he is of me."

Dex raised his glass in silent salute. "I wish for you both a long and happy life together."

"Thank you, Dex. I suspect I'll see a lot of you over the years, seeing you and Nick are such good friends. You'll always be welcomed in our home," Ashley said, stepping close to Nick as he put his arm across her shoulder.

"Hey, old friend, you picked a winner," Dex said, clapping Nick on the other shoulder.

"Mom?" Michelle joined them.

She smiled at Nick and Dex.

"It's time to cut the cake you two, and then you have to get going. Your plane leaves in less than four hours."

As she and her new husband went to cut the wedding cake, Ashley made a mental note to ask Nick later about Dex's comment. But there was too much going on now to have a discussion they probably should have had before.

When it came time to toss the bride's bouquet, Ashley

flipped it over her head, right into the arms of her best friend from work. She laughed when Mary Ellen looked right at Dex. Maybe Nick's friend would be next to the altar.

A half hour later Nick told her it was time to leave. She found Michelle and Charlie near the edge of the group. She gave Charlie big hug, then her daughter.

"Be happy, Mom," she said.

"Take care of her, sir," Charlie said to Nick.

Ashley had to smile, touched Charlie felt the need to be protective.

"I'm sure we'll be as happy as you," Ashley replied.

Michelle made a face.

"At least you and your husband get to make a home together. Charlie still thinks of the Navy ship as home, and it's like he's visiting at our place."

"Hey, Michelle, I explained. It's not like it's forever," Charlie protested.

"Honey, once the next assignment is finished, he could be rotated stateside and you'll be able to get a place together. You ship out soon, don't you?" Ashley asked Charlie.

"In a couple of weeks. Anyway, I'm with you this weekend, Michelle," he said, throwing his arm across her shoulders.

"There is that," she said, smiling at him.

Looking back at Ashley, she said, "We're fine. You have a great time in London. I know you've always wanted to see Big Ben and Westminster Abbey and the Crown Jewels."

Amid a flurry of activity, Nick and Ashley headed for their car. Their bags had been packed before the ceremony. They were ready to drive to the airport and their new life together.

The vague feeling of uncertainty had fled. Committed to making her marriage the best thing in the world, Ashley looked forward to starting her life with Nick. Her rings shone in the light, the diamond and the plain gold circle. They were bound forever. She hoped they'd be as happy forever as they were this day.

It was morning when they landed in London, but Nick wasted no time in sweeping her into their hotel room and into bed. His expertise in making love enthralled Ashley. She had only vague memories of her first husband, but remembered none of the passion and delight she found with Nick.

The long, lonely years had been worth the wait, she thought the next morning, relishing every moment of the night they'd shared. Rolling over in the big bed and finding him there was a pleasure she was sure to repeat for the rest of their lives.

He opened his eyes, drew her close and began to kiss her as if they had all the time in the world. Giving herself to the joy of his touch, Ashley knew she'd found her soul mate.

The days in London flew by. Ashley initially had reservations about a working honeymoon, but Nick made sure he spent as much time as possible with her. When he was tied up with the client, the local firm had a secretary who offered to accompany Ashley wherever she wanted to go. Being London-born and bred, Talia Cummings was the perfect guide.

Though she enjoyed seeing the sights with Talia, Ashley loved the moments shared with Nick the most. They saw a show in the West End, took a carriage ride in Hyde Park, viewed the crown jewels in the Tower of London, and ate cream tea every afternoon.

"I could live here," Ashley said one afternoon as they were wandering through Harrods. "I love London."

"There's still more to see. On our next trip, we can extend ourselves beyond the city," he said. "I thought of transferring here. We could make it our home base for a few years."

"I'd love to see Stonehenge, and the Cotswolds and Hadrian's Wall. Could we really live here? I'd get to see it all."

"Not to mention Scotland and Wales. And it's only a short chunnel trip to reach France."

"Ah, no wonder you are the perfect man, you know how to please a woman."

"Not only traveling, I hope," he said, trailing his finger tips down her cheek.

His touch had her forgetting the chess set she'd been examining and turn to him. Would he think her silly if she suggested they return to their hotel room in the middle of the afternoon?

"No, not only traveling," she replied, remembering their nights together.

Could life be any more perfect?

In the past were the worries she had about raising a child single-handedly, about where to live, how to afford basic necessities. The struggle had paid off, and now she was able to enjoy the reward.

And what a reward it was. Nick and London.

Might as well be daring.

"Want to take a nap?" she asked provocatively.

He smiled that slow smile of his that set her heart to racing. "Sleepy?"

"Not exactly," she said, her eyes holding his, seeing the spark of desire flare.

"Me, either, but I think returning to our room might be a very good thing."

And so it proved to be.

Ashley had never expected life to turn out perfect, yet their week in London seemed to be as perfect as could be.

She wished they could have stayed longer as they boarded the flight back to San Francisco.

"As a honeymoon, this couldn't have been better," she said, snuggling up against Nick as the plane taxied on the runway. "Are you serious about finding a home here?"

"It's something to look into."

What would she do about Michelle?

"If I hadn't had to work, this honeymoon would have been better," he said.

"A few hours here and there. I shopped which you don't like, so as I said, perfect."

"So I should plan to make myself scarce at suitable points on other trips so you can help the local economy?" he asked, brushing his lips against her forehead. His hand tightened its grip on hers. "I wish we were alone on the plane," he said, his dark gaze holding hers. "It's a long flight to San Francisco."

4

When they landed at San Francisco International Airport, it was raining. They passed through customs with no problem and before long were in Nick's sports car heading toward the city.

Ashley was almost asleep. She hadn't slept on the long flight and now had been up more than twenty hours. How had Nick stood it when he'd returned from Amsterdam a couple of weeks ago? She'd have wanted to go straight to bed.

"Where are we going?" she asked.

He glanced at her.

"Home, where else?"

"And that would be your place or mine?"

Despite all the time they'd had since he'd proposed, no firm plans had been made on where they'd live. First she'd rushed through the wedding, then getting her passport, wrapping up as much as she could at work.

Nick had been equally busy after being gone so long from his office. Then they'd taken off for London. How could they have left such a basic discussion remain in abeyance so long? Now the question had to be answered.

"My place tonight. Unless you'd rather go to yours."

"I have a small bed," she said, feeling a bit surreal.

They'd been married a week and neither had seen the

other's bedroom. Did he have a huge bed or a small single like hers?

"I have a king-size one. We'll have to squeeze into my place until we find a place of our own. Unless you'd rather we squeeze into yours."

Ashley considered the prospects, neither a good choice. Her apartment was tiny. At least there were two bedrooms, so it offered a bit more room than Nick's one-bedroom apartment.

She opted for Nick's place. The bed was the selling point. They couldn't both share hers.

Half an hour later he pulled into the parking garage beneath his apartment building. Ashley was almost asleep and had to force herself out of the car. How long until she could be in bed?

They rode the elevator in silence up to his floor. At the door, Nick dropped the suitcases. He unlocked the door, and pushed it open, surprising Ashley by sweeping her off her feet and carrying her across the threshold.

"Wow," she said, laughing up at him.

"Welcome to our home, Mrs. Carstairs," he said, setting her on her feet and kissing her.

Ashley's fatigue fled instantly and she relished the kiss. Nick's very touch was like magic. Winding her arms around his neck, she kissed him back.

When he ended the kiss, he quickly picked up their bags and closed the door to the world.

The next morning Ashley awoke first. She lay snuggled against her husband, marveling at the changes in the last month. She still couldn't believe she was married. That she'd been to London. Unfortunately honeymoons didn't last forever. She had to get into work today. And she knew there'd be a stack of crucial, time sensitive work awaiting.

Her assistant didn't have the experience to deal with the more complex client accounts. And even the ones she could handle, Ashley would still need to review to give her approval.

Slowly she gazed around the bedroom. It was sparse and austere. A bed, a dresser and a night table with a lamp. Would Nick mind when they got a place together if she made it a bit more homey? She didn't like the cluttered look, but she did want a few pictures on the wall.

The view from his place was spectacular. Maybe that's why he didn't have pictures. He hadn't put curtains on the windows. The panoramic view of San Francisco Bay and the Golden Gate Bridge was always a sight she'd never tire of seeing. She hoped they could get a similar view in their new apartment.

"Let's pretend we didn't get back last night," Nick said softly.

She looked at him, thrilled at the desire she saw in his eyes. "And?"

"And stay right here all day."

He drew her closer and kissed her, his hand moving over her, touching her as he'd done so many times during the last week. Every cell went on alert as his caresses turned bolder.

She laughed softly.

"I'd love nothing more, but there's work to be done."

"I knew you'd say that."

He made no move to stop.

"But I don't have to be there until nine," she said suggestively and began to trace patterns against his muscular chest.

"Still too early," he said before his mouth covered hers.

"We need to find a bigger place," Nick said later as they prepared breakfast.

Ashley was trying to find enough food for a meal with the meager supplies in his cupboard. No eggs, cereal or fresh milk. She found some bagels in the freezer and made do with them and some of the cheese she found.

Nick made the coffee, bumping into her more than once. She couldn't tell if it were deliberate or not, but didn't mind a bit.

"Where do you want to live?" she asked.

"Here, only in a bigger unit until we decide about London. I'll check with the manager and see if there is something open on another floor."

"And if not?"

While she liked the idea of moving to London, she wanted to take things slowly. She still had her job to consider. And Michelle.

"Then we'll have to locate another place. How about you? Suggestions?"

"Can we afford the Marina area?"

She'd always loved walking over from her apartment to see the Bay. How terrific to live where she could see the view from her own home. But apartments and houses here were extremely expensive.

He looked at her. "I have enough money to assure we can live wherever you want."

"Oh."

They hadn't discussed finances. In fact they hadn't discussed a lot of basic things. Time enough in the years ahead, she thought.

"I'll check with the manager and if there's nothing open in this building, we'll branch out. I'd like to find a place quickly so we can combine households. It's inefficient to have two separate places."

"I know. I feel like I'm camping out or on a spend-the-night with a friend," she said, reaching for a bagel as it popped up in the toaster.

"And how many spend-the-nights with a friend did you do?" he growled, stopping her hand and swinging her around to face him.

The teasing lights in his eyes had her smiling.

"None since Michelle was born. But Jenny Knight and I used to take turns all the time in high school."

"Girlfriends?" he said.

"You thought boyfriends?" she teased, surprised at the hint of jealousy that showed in his face.

"Why wouldn't I? You're beautiful, fun to be around, sexy, intriguing. Why wouldn't the men be swarming at your feet?"

She wrinkled her nose.

"Most men don't swarm around a mother with a little child to care for."

"Ah, then my timing was excellent. Another week, what with Michelle married off, and the swarm would have begun."

She laughed and reached up to kiss him. She loved this wildly sexy man and his flattering speech.

A week away was either too much or not nearly enough, Ashley thought as she walked into her office at nine. She had more work than she thought she'd ever get through. Maybe she shouldn't have taken off until after the tax deadline. Time away from the office at this point hadn't been such a great idea. Now she had to pay the piper.

"Ah, Ashley," Mr. Popovich stepped into the doorway.

Ashley smiled at her boss.

"Hello, sir. Managed fine without me, I see," she said, placing her purse in the top drawer as normal.

"Not at all, my dear. I've asked your assistant to bring you up to speed as soon as you're ready. There's probably more than you'll be expecting, but to tell the truth there aren't many accountants here in the firm I trust as much as I do you," he said.

He glanced at the stack of folders on her desk.

"I hope you realize what a valued employee you are," he said.

A small smile touched his lips.

"Actually, maybe it's even better that I realize what a valued employee you are. I'm glad you're back."

"Thank you, it's good to be back."

Ashley called her assistant in and they began to review what had transpired during the last week.

Occasionally during the day, Ashley thought about the week in London. It already seemed like a dream. Only the stack of financial records in front of her seemed real.

Ashley was still working at six that evening when her cell phone rang.

"Mom? I didn't know if you were back or not. I left you several messages. Didn't you get them?" Michelle's voice came across the line.

"Hi, honey. I think my phone is still on silence. I've been totally swamped today. We got in last night and stayed at Nick's place."

Ashley leaned back against her chair, tired enough to call it quits, but with more she wanted to finish before calling it a day.

"Too late to call?" Michelle said. "Was your flight late?"

Oops. No they hadn't gotten in too late to call, but any thought of contacting her daughter had fled when Nick kissed her.

How could a mother explain that?

"Sorry. Don't worry, you can tell we got home safely. How are you?"

"Fine. Did you have fun?" Michelle asked.

"Yes. London was magical."

She'd enjoyed every moment spent with her new husband. Thinking of Nick made her warm all over.

She pushed aside the folder she'd been working on. It could wait. As soon as she was finished talking with Michelle, she was heading home.

"Want to get together for dinner or lunch or something this week?" Michelle asked.

"Is something wrong?"

Ashley immediately switched back into Mom mode.

Michelle laughed.

"No, Mom, nothing's wrong. I want to hear all about being married and your honeymoon in London, that's all. Of course, if you can't spare the time, I'd understand. Being a newly wed and all."

"Lunch tomorrow," Ashley said firmly, marking it on her calendar. She remembered Friday was the day Michelle didn't have classes.

"Meet me at the Pelican Roost on Montgomery Street at eleven-thirty and we'll beat the rush."

"Okay. Tell my new dad hi for me."

Ashley smiled at the nonsense. She could just imagine Nick's face if Michelle really started calling him Dad. He'd said he couldn't picture himself as a father. She couldn't either. He was too exciting and free a man to be a father who played ball with his kids or attended school functions.

Nick stood at the window gazing out at the Bay. It was dark, after six, and where the heck was Ashley? He'd tried her cell earlier, but she hadn't answered. Obviously the switchboard had closed for the night.

She needed to remember she was married now and had someone worrying about her when she wasn't where he thought she should be.

He knew he was being impatient. There'd be a period of adjustment for them both. She worked long hours at tax time, she'd told him that. But hearing it and experiencing it were two different things.

He wanted her home with him.

He'd have taken her with him to work if he could have done so.

First thing tonight, he wanted to discuss her giving up her

job so they could be together when he was free. No time like the present to quit. There was plenty to do with finding a new apartment and getting settled.

He still considered making London their base, but she'd asked for time—still watching over her daughter.

Michelle was married and he suspected didn't need her mother's watchful eye. It wouldn't be long before Ashley would want to move. He could be patient in the meantime. He hoped.

He heard the key in the lock. His feeling of anticipation soared. Turning, he crossed the room swiftly, flinging wide the door and looking at her.

She was so beautiful his teeth almost ached. She smiled broadly and stepped into his arms, lifting her mouth for his kiss. Wildly Nick wondered if she'd be willing to postpone dinner while they detoured through the bedroom.

"I thought you were never coming home," he said a few moments later when Ashley dropped a heavy briefcase on the chair and shrugged out of her coat.

"I still have tons of work to do. But I wanted to get home to you," she said, brushing his cheek with her fingers.

He caught her hand and kissed her palm, needing some contact with her. He'd never expected to feel this loss when she was absent. Nor feel connected somehow when she was with him.

"I don't have any more food in the house tonight than we did this morning. We'll have to go out to dinner," he said, hoping she'd rather order in.

"Is that your normal way, eat out all the time?" she asked, kicking off her shoes.

"Yeah, works for me."

"Well, now you have a wife who enjoys cooking, so we don't have to go out all the time. I want to change my clothes before we do anything," she said heading for the bedroom.

If she had to get out of those clothes anyway.

He followed her into the bedroom.

Some time later Nick drove to a small Chinese restaurant on Lombard Street.

As they were eating, Ashley said, "I have to stop by my apartment and get some more clothes."

"Fine."

As long as she didn't stay at that apartment, they could stop there as often as she wanted. He liked having her in his place. And in his bed.

"We also need to stop at the supermarket for some food," she added.

"Tonight?" he asked.

"Yes. What were you planning to have for breakfast if we don't get something?"

"We could eat out."

"Are you made of money?" she asked.

Nick went quiet. They'd never discussed finances in any detail. He suspected Ashley hadn't a clue how much money he did have. Aste was a huge success. He and Dex and Tony had made millions the first five years in business. And he hadn't spent much of it. Even if he quit work today, he'd have enough invested to live comfortably for the rest of his life. More than comfortably.

He reached for her hand.

"Ashley, I have enough money to cover any expenses we

come up with. If we want to eat out every meal, we can. If we want to hire a cook for our meals, that'll work. If you want to cook, that's fine by me, but only if you want to."

She stared at him for a long moment, then shook her head.

"I'm not sure I can comprehend that," she said. "For so long I've pinched pennies to make ends meet. It was so hard when Michelle was little. We didn't live in a nice neighborhood or have enough money for the toys I wished I could have given her. Sometimes I had to walk to school and then to work because I couldn't even afford bus fare."

"You don't have money worries now," Nick said.

"No, I don't. I make a good income, but I still watch where we spend the money."

"I meant, with me," he said.

He certainly couldn't accuse Ashley of being a gold digger. She seemed to have a hard time remembering they were married, a couple who shared everything. He didn't need his wife to work. And she need never worry about money again.

"Oh."

"I wanted you to know so you won't worry about quitting your job."

"Quitting my job?" she repeated.

He nodded.

"We talked about it, remember? So you can travel with me."

"I remember."

"But?"

Nick didn't like the stubborn look that appeared. Nor did he like it when she withdrew her hand.

"But not yet," she said, beginning to eat again.

"Why not? I'll be getting another assignment soon. Who knows where, but you'll want to go, right?"

She nodded.

"If I can get time off."

"If you can get time off? Take the time. Quit the blasted job and come with me."

"You don't know that you'll get an assignment soon. Besides, I can't leave the company in the lurch at this time of year. You know it's the busiest time."

Her tone was reasonable, but he didn't like what she was saying.

"They'll find another accountant."

"My boss told me today how valued an employee I am."

"He's undoubtedly right about that. Should have told you long ago."

And paid her more. Heck, made her a partner. No, not that. A partnership would be hard to leave.

"Maybe my being away helped him realize that," she said, smiling. "Eat up, Nick. We can discuss this later. We still have to visit the supermarket, don't forget."

Nick ate the remainder of his meal in silence, studying his new wife. That conversation had not gone the way he wanted. He'd thought she'd be thrilled to learn money was not an issue. Be glad to quit her job and plan their next trip together.

Instead she acted almost as if he was being unreasonable expecting her to give up the work to travel. Which is what she said she wanted.

Women. He knew he'd never understand them. Where was the logic in her thinking?

Ashley ate, forcing the food down. It tasted like cardboard. She tried to keep a bright smile on her face, but it was an effort. She felt panic at the thought of quitting her job. She'd worked so hard to put herself through college, get her degree and then the job at the firm. How could she just quit?

What would happen to her if Nick left?

The thought stunned her.

She looked at her plate, not seeing the egg rolls and sweet and sour pork, but seeing Darrell walk out on her and Michelle. Seeing the years of struggle with no help to speak of. The fear that had lived with her for so long that she'd be destitute.

How could she fear Nick would leave? The circumstances were totally different. He wasn't some young boy just out of high school, but a man who knew his own mind. She wasn't the uneducated mother of an infant struggling to make ends meet.

Still, the need for security proved stronger than she expected. It was one thing for him to say he had money, something else for her to be dependent on his money.

What if he left?

"I'm finished," she said, pushing away the plate.

Her appetite had fled. The happiness that had bubbled around her for weeks evaporated.

For the first time she took a long look at where she was and what she'd done.

She'd married a man she hardly knew. So far married life had been perfect. What happened when it didn't go as they wanted? How would they weather hard times–united or divided?

Dare she risk her security on a man she'd met only weeks ago?

She loved Nick, but as she watched him summon the waiter and settle the bill, it struck her he'd never told her he loved her.

Don't be silly, she scolded herself as they walked out of the restaurant. Of course he loved her. Hadn't he proved that a dozen ways? Men were not as free with emotional revelations as women. Just because he hadn't said the words didn't mean anything. Obviously not, since tonight was the first time she'd realized the lack.

"Where to first, your place or the supermarket?" he asked as he held the car door.

"My place. We'll see what I have on hand that we can take to your apartment and then I'll know more what to get at the store."

"*Our* apartment," he growled.

"Oops, sorry," she apologized.

Touchy, wasn't he? It'd take a while to adjust to being married, she thought.

And the sooner they found a place that was theirs, the easier it would be.

No matter what he said, the apartment felt like it was his. As her place was hers. He didn't even want to stay at her apartment, at least she'd compromised enough to agree to move into his until they found a larger place.

The next morning Ashley was swamped. Her work seemed to have multiplied overnight and she wondered if she slept in her office, she'd find gremlins mass producing new accounts at midnight each night.

Despite the increase in workload, she left in plenty of time to meet Michelle for lunch. The week and a day since the wedding was one of the longest stretches she'd been apart from her daughter. She missed her. She'd thought it'd be cool to live in London, but now she wasn't sure. Michelle would be so far away.

They didn't have to decide immediately.

Today, she wanted to catch up on all her news, how her classes were going, if she and Charlie had heard any more about where his next posting would be. To see if she had any questions now as a married woman she hadn't had before.

Ashley arrived before Michelle and picked a quiet table in the back. Waving when she spotted her daughter, she rose and hugged her.

"It's so good to see you, honey," she said, brushing back Michelle's blond hair, windblown from the breeze.

"It's great to see you, Mom. Wow, you look ten years younger. Being married must agree with you."

"With Nick it does," Ashley confirmed, sitting at the table.

When Michelle slid into the seat across from her, Ashley studied her.

"You look tired, honey."

"A bit. The quarter will be ending soon and I'm studying for finals."

Once their order had been placed, Ashley smiled at her daughter.

"Beyond school, how's married life?"

Ashley asked, expecting a glowing report, like the one she'd give if asked.

"Okay. Not what I thought it would be," Michelle said, studying the menu.

"Only okay?"

Never in her wildest dreams could Ashley quantify her marriage as *okay*. She missed Nick. It had been less than four hours since she was with him, and she missed him. Even the difference of opinion last night had been a small blip on the great scheme of happiness. As if he were making up for something, their lovemaking had been fantastic.

"Actually, I hardly feel married. Charlie's on base all the time. He spends the weekends with me, but says it's too much trouble to fight the traffic to get to our place during the week, when he has to be on duty so early the next morning."

Michelle sipped her water and looked around the restaurant. Looking back at her mother, she shrugged.

"I guess I thought it would be fireworks. Instead I'm still studying and he's still in the Navy. He ships out in another week."

"It'll be different when you two live together," Ashley said, wondering why Charlie wasn't pushing to make sure he and Michelle spent as much time together as possible before he had to leave. They'd be apart for six months when he left.

"I know. When he gets his next duty station, I hope we're posted somewhere away from California," Michelle said.

"What?"

Ashley had known there was a big possibility they'd be posted outside California. She didn't want to think about not being close to Michelle.

But to hear her daughter say it surprised her.

"Phyllis is driving me crazy. She's forever stopping over and bringing goodies, as if I don't know how to cook or something. *Charlie loves my brownies, or Charlie can't get enough of my lemon meringue pie.* Sheesh, he hardly eats at our place anyway. We go out on the weekends and he's at the base the rest of the time."

"He's her only son, she's probably glad he's back for a while and wants to do things for him," Ashley said gently, remembering how overprotective Phyllis Stratford could be.

Their food was served and they began to eat.

Michelle looked at her mother and smiled.

"So, tell me about being married to that hunk and how your honeymoon was."

"It's terrific. And the honeymoon was wonderful. We saw Big Ben and heard it chime. Toured Westminster Abbey and the Houses of Parliament. Did you know they bury people right in the walkways of the church? I rode a double decker bus and—"

"Mom," Michelle said, laughing. "I don't want a sightseeing guide, I want to hear detail about you and Nick."

"X-rated," Ashley said with satisfaction.

"Wow," Michelle's expression picked up. "Tell all."

"I hardly think it's appropriate," Ashley said, then giggled. "Oh, my, if I had had any idea what I'd been missing all those years, I would have started dating when you were one."

"I doubt you would have found many men like Nick Carstairs," Michelle said dryly. "He seems one of a kind to me."

"I believe you're right," Ashley said, knowing she had a sappy smile on her face.

Merely thinking about the man made her insides tingle and her heart pound. She glanced at her watch. Another six hours until she saw him again.

It was closer to eight hours later when Nick arrived home. Ashley beat him by more than an hour. She'd changed and prepared dinner. When he hadn't arrived by seven, she began to worry. When he opened the door, she felt a wave of relief.

"I thought you'd gotten lost," she said, running to meet him.

"Tough day," he said, drawing her into his embrace and kissing her.

Then he lifted his head and sniffed.

"Something smells terrific and it isn't just you."

"Nothing fancy, just spaghetti and meatballs, garlic bread and salad. This weekend we need to stock up on your pantry. Our pantry," she quickly corrected herself.

This was their place, until they found another. She needed to remember that.

He took off his jacket and tossed it on the sofa.

"I won't be here this weekend. Pack your bags, sweetheart, we're off to Paris."

"Paris?"

Her favorite dream, visiting that old city, walking along the Seine, riding up the Eiffel Tower and seeing the entire City of Lights spread before her.

"I can't."

The disappointment was tangible.

"What do you mean, you can't? You said you wanted to see Paris."

"I do, but I can't ask for more time off. I've had two weeks in the last month. This is our busy season. I can't expect the others to shoulder my workload."

"Quit the darn job."

"It's my career," she said with dignity. "I'm not asking you to give up yours."

"Mine pays a lot more and offers perks yours could never dream of. I thought you wanted to be footloose and fancy-free going where we could when we could."

"I do. But to quit my job right at tax time? I can't do it."

"Independence is a fine thing, sweetheart. I admire you for all you've done with your life. But live a little. Come with me," he coaxed.

She was so tempted. But doubts rose.

She knew they'd talked about her leaving her job and going with him when he went on assignments, but somehow she'd thought of it more like daydreaming. Or long vacations from work. She hadn't really thought it through. It was a huge change. Not something she could do on the spur of the moment.

What if something happened? She'd need a way to support herself. She had a good job, with seniority, the respect of her boss and coworkers. She couldn't chuck it all for a fling in Paris.

"I can't."

"Can't? Or won't?" he asked.

"Not yet. I've worked hard to get where I am. I can't just leave it all behind with no warning and no notice."

"We planned to travel, to see the world together. That's what you said you wanted."

He had a hard edge to his voice.

"I do want that. I can get more time off after April, really."

"So you'll skip Paris for a bunch of tax forms?"

"I'm sure you'll go again before we die," she said,

struggling to keep from throwing herself into his arms and agreeing to anything he wanted.

"Can't you see my side of it?" she asked.

"No," he said. "I have money, that's not an issue. You said you wanted to travel, so what's the deal? You don't need a career, unless it's professional traveler. Which you'll never be staying home all the time to do other people's taxes."

The buzzer sounded in the kitchen. Ashley whirled around, glad for the distraction.

How could she fully explain her need to keep her career going without giving away her greatest fear that he'd leave her one day exactly as her first husband had?

5

Ashley had to give Nick credit for not belaboring the point. He tried once more at dinner to convince her to come with him to Paris. When she refused, he dropped the subject, saying only he had to leave the next afternoon.

"I'm sorry," she said again.

" Okay, then. You're right, Paris will always be there. I had one of the secretaries at the firm run down a list of places for rent in our neighborhood. Want to go over that tonight?"

"Yes."

Anything to cover the disappointment she felt. She was so torn--stay and keep her career as a buffer against what might never happen or splurge and go.

What happened to the new woman--daring and adventuresome?

She was too cautious.

As soon as their few dinner dishes were washed and put away, Ashley joined Nick on the sofa, looking at the listings. They discussed the locations of several apartments. Ashley couldn't help noticing the exorbitant rents. She bit her tongue, not saying a word.

He'd made it clear he could afford this, she wouldn't make an issue of it. But she was stunned at how much money they'd be spending each month. She'd better keep her job and maybe push for a raise.

"We can go to take a look at these in the morning," he said a little while later, indicating the ones they'd circled as being the most suitable on paper at least.

She wanted to see them personally before deciding anything.

"Let's get up early then," she suggested.

"Good idea," he said, drawing her into his arms. "Which means we should get to bed soon, right?" He nuzzled her neck, causing shivers of excitement.

The next morning they ate breakfast at a bakery near the apartment. The warm croissants were huge, light and delicious. Ashley could have stayed all morning, but they were on a schedule. Nick was leaving that afternoon for Paris.

Once finished eating, they headed for the first listing on their sheet. The place had a great location, but no view.

Ashley shook her head at one point and Nick picked up on it quickly. He thanked the manager showing the place and they headed for number two.

By early afternoon, Nick began checking his watch.

"Is time getting short? " Ashley asked, noticing.

She felt a clutch of panic. She didn't want him to leave.

She wished she was going with him.

"This is the last one we have time to see today. I've got to get home and pack. My plane leaves at six."

Ashley paused in the lobby of the building.

"Then, let's skip this one and go home now. I don't want to see any more today. I didn't realize how hard it would be to find something we both like. I was so glad to get my current apartment when I did that I never considered how lucky it was to get what I could afford as well as liked. Too bad we couldn't rent the apartment next to yours and knock out a wall."

"We'll find something. This is only the first day. You can look at these others while I'm gone. If you like one, we'll go together as soon as I get back."

She nodded, still feeling the pang of disappointment that he was leaving so soon after they returned home from London. She should have expected it, Nick had told her sometimes he barely had time to change clothes before heading out again. She'd seen evidence of that first hand in Tahoe.

He seemed to thrive on the challenges, but she wondered if she could adapt to such uncertainties. She realized she liked the routine of her job, of her daily habits. Maybe she'd been fooling herself that she was a footloose kind of person.

All too soon he was gone. Ashley sat in the empty living room and wondered what she was going to do with the rest of the weekend. Shopping held no appeal. Nor did seeing apartments without him.

If she were home, there'd be plenty to do.

Maybe she should return to her own place. She could start packing for the move, get rid of things she didn't need. Make sure all perishables were taken care of.

The knock on the door surprised her. She wasn't expecting anyone.

Opening the door, Ashley came face-to-face with a young, busty blonde wearing a tight dark blue shirt and painted-on jeans.

"Hi, is Nick here?" the woman asked.

"No, he's on his way to Paris."

"That lucky guy. He's always going somewhere fabulous isn't he? Are you his latest?"

"Latest?"

"Girlfriend. I'm Leslie White. He and I were an item a few months ago. I think I left my favorite lipstick here. I can't find it anywhere and remember using it once when I was here."

Ashley stared at her.

"I haven't seen it," she said.

Leslie tilted her head slightly.

"It might be in the bathroom, or in the bedside table. I could take a quick look."

"Come in."

Ashley stepped aside and closed the door behind her unexpected guest. She watched as Leslie walked straight through to the bathroom, and a moment later headed for the bedroom.

Ashley followed. It was obvious Leslie knew her away around the apartment. Just how close had she and Nick been?

Ashley felt a pang of jealousy. This woman was young, trim and pretty. She moved with such assurance. For a moment, Ashley could picture Nick and Leslie together.

She frowned. That was in the past. Nick was married to her now.

"Nope, not either place," Leslie said with a frown.

She looked at Ashley again.

"Are you staying here? I saw some girly stuff in the bathroom. Nick usually doesn't use pink razors."

"Nick and I are married."

Ashley should have told her that at the beginning.

"Married? Nick? No way. I don't believe it."

The surprise on Leslie's face was almost comical.

"A week ago Thursday," Ashley said, resisting the urge to wave her wedding ring in front of Leslie's nose. The younger woman was stunning, her eyes large and expressive, her long hair a pale blond, nothing like her own honey-brown color.

"I never thought I'd see the day. If I'd ever believed he'd settle down, I'd have tried harder. Good for you catching him."

"I didn't catch him," Ashley said.

Leslie crossed her arms over her rather large chest and looked around.

"I never thought he'd stay still long enough to get married. He's always going somewhere. But we had fun when he was here. Darn, I wish I knew where my lipstick was. They don't make that color anymore and I loved it."

"If I find it, I'll be sure to let you know," Ashley said, trying not to picture Nick with this younger woman.

He'd chosen *her* to marry, not Leslie or anyone else.

But it was hard not to compare herself and her conservative clothes to this beautiful, trendy, younger woman.

"Thanks. Hey, tell Nick congrats for me, will you?" Leslie headed for the front door. "He'll know where to find me if you do find the lipstick."

She left and Ashley remained standing where she was.

She'd heard Dex call him a playboy, and for a moment, she'd been thrilled someone like that would single her out. Now she wasn't sure how she felt coming face to face with someone from Nick's past.

Rational thought dictated she let it go. But she couldn't

help comparing the other woman to herself and coming up short.

What had Nick seen in her that caused him to offer marriage? Some of it was the spark of attraction, she knew that. And he'd said he'd always wanted someone to travel with him.

She'd let him down on that front, refusing to go to Paris. It was hard letting go of what was familiar and comfortable.

Not liking her thoughts, she grabbed her jacket and headed to the apartment that had been home for the last nine years.

Ashley spent the night at her old place surrounded by familiar things. As she drifted to sleep, she could almost imagine the last month had been a dream and she'd wake up in the morning back to her old routine.

The next morning, she began to pack. By noon her bedroom and the living room were denuded of pictures and knickknacks and books–everything packed into some boxes she'd found.

She loaded her car with clothes and headed back to Nick's apartment. She and Michelle would have to arrange a time to go through the rest of the apartment together. Michelle had left most of her things in her room when she rented the apartment she shared with Charlie.

Ashley wanted to get an apartment with a guest room so Michelle and Charlie could visit if they ended up being assigned to another other state.

Nick had seemed agreeable enough when she brought it up. Only shaking his head again when he looked at her, teasingly telling her he was still amazed she could be the mother of a grown child.

She'd teased him back calling him Dad, and laughed aloud when he'd looked almost hunted.

"Never pictured myself as a father," he'd said gruffly.

"What did you picture yourself when you were a child?" she'd asked.

"A pirate for the most part or a marshal in an old west town. Until I discovered computers. Then I was set for life."

When Ashley arrived at his apartment, the answering machine was blinking. Nick's strong voice came across when she pushed the button.

"Ashley?" He'd waited a couple of seconds. "Are you there? I'm at my hotel. I tried your cell but didn't get an answer. So I'm calling this hoping you'll hear the message. Call me when you get this."

He rattled off a string of numbers. Ashley quickly found a pad and paper in her purse and wrote them down as he talked for a few minutes longer, obviously hoping she'd pick up.

Darn. She hadn't thought about his calling when he reached Paris. He probably wondered where she was. Calculating the time difference, she realized it was after midnight in Paris, too late to call tonight.

She played the message again, delighting in hearing his voice. She wished she'd been home to talk to him.

She checked her cell. It was dead. She'd forgotten to charge it. She did that a lot, since she didn't use the phone much.

Ashley called Nick the next morning, but he'd already left the hotel. She had to use the land line since she didn't have world wide coverage on her cell phone.

"Probably working," she murmured to herself as she sipped her morning coffee. It was late afternoon in Paris. She'd try calling from work later.

Despite calling almost every hour and incurring a huge phone bill on the company's line, Ashley didn't reach Nick.

By the time she arrived home, she was frustrated at not connecting. Where was he? Had he been this annoyed with her when she wasn't home yesterday?

She dialed once again. She didn't care about the time difference, she wanted to talk to him.

"'Lo," a sleepy voice answered.

"Sorry I missed your call yesterday," she said, feeling complete now that she heard him again. She sank into the chair and closed her eyes, imagining him next to her.

"Hi sweetheart. I got your messages. I tried to call earlier but someone said you were in a meeting."

"I didn't get that message. How are you? Sorry to wake you up. *I miss you,*" she said.

"I'm glad you did. I miss you, too. You should have come, the weather's incredible for March. Flowers are blooming all over the place and nothing's crowded as most tourists don't venture forth this early in the year."

"I wish I had, too," she said, wondering how long she could stand to be away from him. "The weather's nice here, too. In fact, they're predicting an unusual warm spell for the next week. It seems like it's later in the year rather than only early spring."

"I should wrap things up by Thursday and head for home then. How about I see if we can borrow Tony's sailboat. We'll go sailing on Saturday if the weather holds."

"Sounds like fun."

"Where were you when I called yesterday?" he asked.

"I was at my place packing. I need to get Michelle over to help go through things, but we can do that once you and I find an apartment and know when we can move."

"Did you look at any more apartments?"

"No, it didn't seem right without you."

"If we go sailing on Saturday, we can spend Sunday looking."

"Okay. I miss you, Nick."

She didn't care if she sounded needy, she wanted him to know how much she missed him.

She almost ached with a longing that frightened her. He'd become such an integral part of her life so quickly. She wasn't used to being so involved with anyone.

"I miss you, too, sweetheart. Next time, plan to come with me. There are so many things I wanted to show you. You'll love Paris."

"I want to see it all."

"Just not until taxes are done," he said dryly.

She smiled. Maybe he did understand.

"Right. Oh, you had a friend stop by," she said, remembering Leslie. "She was looking for a lipstick she thought she might have left here."

He didn't say anything right away. Ashley wished she'd kept her mouth shut. But she'd started this.

"Her name was Leslie White."

"Sorry she bothered you. I don't think she left anything there."

His tone was distant, no longer warm and intimate.

"We didn't find it, but I told her I'd contact her if it showed up. She said you knew how to reach her."

"She works at a company we do business with. We dated for a while. She's not someone to worry about," he said.

"Umm."

She wished she didn't feel jealous, but couldn't help it. At least he never need know.

"Have a great trip and hurry home," she said wanting to change the subject.

"I'll call you tomorrow night about this time."

"No, it's late where you are."

"But we can't talk while you're at work. And I'm not waiting till Thursday to hear your voice again. I'll call tomorrow."

She hung up after he said goodnight.

She should have gone with him. Nick was nothing like her first husband. The circumstances were totally different. He wasn't going to walk out on her. She had to believe that.

While she was wishing, she wished she hadn't seen the pretty girl he'd once dated. Still, she couldn't shake the nagging worry that one day he'd wake up and be horrified at what he'd done and leave.

Thursday Ashley was on tenterhooks waiting for Nick to get home. She could hardly concentrate on work. Time after time she checked her watch, trying to calculate when his plane would land. She hoped she beat him home. She couldn't wait.

Suddenly there was a commotion outside her office. She looked up to see her husband come striding through the doorway.

"Nick."

She pushed back from her desk and jumped up, running to greet him.

"I told Stacey you'd be glad for the interruption," he said, as she reached him.

He pulled her into his arms and kissed her long and deep. The office faded, the work vanished, there was only Nick and the feel of him in her arms, his hard body pressed against hers, his mouth doing wonderful things with hers. His arms holding her as if he'd never let her go.

"I don't know how many of these trips I want to take with you here and me across the world," he said a few minutes later when he reluctantly ended the kiss. He rested his forehead against hers.

Ashley clung to his shoulders, afraid her knees wouldn't hold her. He had the power to turn her bones into mush.

She couldn't say anything to reassure him, not yet. She'd given the situation a lot of thought during the days he'd been gone. She decided she'd give notice once the tax season ended. Feeling grateful to the firm for giving her her first job and the promotions that had moved her into her current position, she didn't want to leave them at a critical time.

But she wanted to share Nick's life and if that meant traveling the world, then she was all for it.

"It's been endless. I'm so glad to see you."

He brushed his mouth across hers.

"Can you leave now?" he asked.

"Yes. Let me get my purse."

She didn't even tidy up her desk, but grabbed her purse and headed for the door.

"I'll be back in the morning," she told Stacey.

"You two have fun," her assistant said with a wide grin.

"I took the bus so I didn't have to worry about parking. I can ride home with you," Ashley said as they descended in the elevator.

"Want to eat out tonight?" Nick asked, linking his hand with hers, lacing their fingers. "I'm all for a quick meal and then home to bed."

"Sounds great."

She squeezed his fingers, wondering what he'd say if she suggested they skip dinner.

Nick arranged with his partner Tony to borrow his sailboat Saturday and that morning, Ashley woke with a feeling of excited anticipation. She looked forward to speeding across the Bay in the sleek craft since he'd first suggested the idea. She dressed warmly. Despite the sunshine and balmy temperatures for March, it'd be cool on the water.

When they reached the marina, Ashley was surprised at the sleek, elegant boat. The mast towered above them. It was spacious, yet small enough for two to handle. When Nick gave her a tour, she found it had all the amenities of home.

After exploring the interior, she stepped out on the deck where Nick was studying charts. The gentle motion of the boat made her feel a little queasy, but she ignored it. This was another new adventure. She'd have many to come with Nick. She wanted to explore everything that came her way.

"Aren't we just going around the Bay? Isn't it deep enough for the boat or are there channels we have to stay in?" she asked, looking over his shoulder at the charts with the squiggly lines.

He turned and pulled her close with an arm over her shoulders.

"The Bay is surprisingly shallow in many spots. Not enough for the sandy bottom to poke up from the water, but enough we could drag a sandbar if we didn't know where we're going. I thought we'd sail to Sausalito and have lunch there. Maybe go out beneath the Golden Gate Bridge later."

She looked across the expanse of water at the large nature preserve called Angel Island. They'd sail close to that on the way to Sausalito. Maybe even see deer from the boat.

"Sounds great. What shall I do?"

Nick gave her very basic instructions and before long they cast off.

Ashley had little to do once they were under way and sat near Nick, enjoying the wind blowing through her hair.

She still felt a bit queasy and tried to ignore the fact, but when they left the shelter of the marina, it grew rough. Tiny whitecaps topped the waves as they skimmed along, moving up and down as they headed for the Island.

Soon Ashley was unable to do anything but try to concentrate on not being sick.

"Are you all right?" Nick asked, glancing at her.

"I will be," she said, taking another deep breath of the clean air.

She couldn't be a bad sailor. This was something Nick loved. She wanted to do everything they could together. She'd get her sea legs soon, she simply had to.

"You look green."

"Oh."

With that, she dashed to the side of the boat and lost her breakfast.

"Ashley?"

She spun around.

Nick looked in at her. "Are you seasick?"

"I think so. I feel better now. You should be steering the boat."

Visions of them crashing into something rose.

"I dropped the sails. We'll drift for a bit, but there's nothing nearby. I didn't expect you'd be seasick," he said. "I'll see if Tony keeps any remedies around."

"It's my first time on a sailboat, I didn't know I'd react this way. I'm feeling better already," she said, embarrassed to be a problem on a day that had started out so promising.

"Want to head back?"

She shook her head, feeling miserable.

"No. I'll conquer this, let's keep on to Sausalito. I can get something there for the return trip."

In a short time Nick had the boat flying toward the Marin coast and the quaint, arty town of Sausalito. Ashley stood near the rail, watching the distant horizon. She'd read somewhere that watching the horizon helped with seasickness. Only, it didn't seem to be working. She still felt awful.

She greeted their arrival with relief. Stepping on the dock, she took another deep breath, hoping the queasiness would fade now that she was on dry land.

In only moments, she felt marginally better.

"I thought we could eat at a sushi bar near here," Nick said after the boat was secured in the slip.

The thought of fish almost made Ashley's stomach revolt again.

"No. Not yet. I think I need to find my sea legs before I

could face fish. What I think I'd like is someplace where I could get a cup of soup."

"There are a lot of restaurants within walking distance from here. We'll find something to suit you." he said, throwing his arm around her shoulders and heading toward land.

They wandered around the small village, perusing menus, commenting on the outdoor cafes. Ashley took time to look over her shoulder at the skyline of San Francisco now and then. The air felt cool blowing from the Bay, but the sun kept the temperatures comfortable.

As she walked, she began to feel better. She dreaded the return trip, however.

Another disappointment. Maybe she wasn't as ready for life on the wild side. She hoped Nick wasn't too unhappy.

She felt as if her plans were being extinguished one by one.

Nick took Ashley's hand and headed up Bridgeway Street. He was disappointed she didn't take to sailing like he did. Tony rarely used his boat since his marriage. His wife's sister was wheelchair-bound, so they didn't go often. Tony made it available to Nick and Dex whenever they wanted it. Nick thought about taking Ashley sailing for an extended time, maybe taking a trip down to Monterey or up to Fort Bragg.

But if she was bothered by the light chop in the Bay, she'd never survive the larger swells of the Pacific.

They passed a deli and he stopped.

"They have soup and sandwiches, let's try this," he suggested.

She smiled and nodded.

"Let's eat on the patio," she said, nodding toward the

outdoor tables and chairs on the side patio.

He couldn't gauge if she was feeling better or just putting on a good face. He stopped her before they entered, resting his hands on her shoulders.

"If you're not feeling well, I can call Dex or Tony or someone to come get the boat. We don't have to take the boat back."

"Actually I'm feeling much better. I'm sorry to be such a wet blanket. I never thought I'd be the type to get seasick."

"Maybe you just need to get used to sailing."

"I guess."

He was struck once again by how pretty she was when she looked up, her eyes dark with concern.

"I really want to do this," she said. "I loved it when we started out."

"Give it time. If sailing doesn't agree with you, we'll try something else."

He loved the freedom of the boat. If he were in town longer between assignments, he might have considered getting his own. But the upkeep was too much with his erratic schedule. Still, he hoped it might be something they could enjoy together.

"Let's eat and I'll see how I feel," she said.

After lunch, Ashley declared she was fine. They wandered around the shops in the quaint little community. Nick bought ice cream for them and they sat in one of the many little parks, enjoying the view of the Bay and City. He didn't push about the return trip, but if she needed someone else to take back the boat, he wanted to call them soon.

She enjoyed everything they'd done since landing. He

glanced around. Normally he wouldn't have spent so much time in such a tourist spot. But with Ashley, he saw it with different eyes.

The town was clean and fresh and pretty with all the flowers and mini parks. With the bright sunshine, and the fresh breeze, the day was ideal. Slowly he began to relax. He'd never have suspected a month or two ago that he'd be married and content to spend a day doing virtually nothing.

"Ready to go?" she asked, tossing her napkin in the nearby trash barrel.

"Want me to call someone to come get the boat?"

"Nope, I'm ready to sail the seas again." She smiled and stood. "Come on, Captain, our ship awaits."

Nick was relieved to see her enjoying herself on the return trip. It wasn't quite as rough with the wind behind them and Ashley even asked for a turn at the helm. He stood close by, not just to help, but from a need to be within touching distance. He'd only known her a few weeks, but somehow it seemed like forever. He wasn't one to analyze relationships. Usually he'd been more the love 'em and leave 'em type.

But Ashley was different. Around her, he was different.

He watched as San Francisco came closer. Tomorrow they'd go apartment hunting again. He hoped they'd find something they both liked. With most of her things still at her apartment, it felt as if she was merely visiting his.

She still stumbled over the his and ours when talking about the apartment.

He knew she was adjusting to marriage as he was. But he had no problem thinking of it as their place. Of thinking of Ashley at home when he was away.

"This is great," she called, laughing at the fun of it.

She looked at the dock, coming faster than expected.

"Oh, yikes. What do we do now? Are we going to crash?"

"We furl the sails and take it in under power," Nick said, moving to begin the process.

It was going to be all right. She had her sea legs now and they could do this more and more as the summer took hold.

Working together, Ashley questioning every step, they secured the sails and headed for the slip under power.

When they docked, she flung her arms around his neck.

"That was so much fun. I think I got my sea legs on the return trip. Can we do it again soon?"

He swung her around, liking the feel of her soft feminine body against his. He glanced toward the cabin, calculating whether they could use it or if he could wait for her until they got home.

"As long as Tony isn't using it. We could take a longer sail next weekend. Maybe even head out under the bridge."

"Wow, on the ocean? Let's explore around the Bay some more before we go there. I don't want to chance my luck."

He looked at her for a long moment. Her eyes were sparkling, her smile infectious and her cheeks kissed by the sun and wind to a rosy hue. He'd like to see her always so excited and happy.

They found the perfect apartment the next afternoon, two bedrooms, a large living room and a kitchen big enough for them to move around together without bumping into each other. It was only two blocks from Nick's current one and had a view that matched. Since it was already vacant, they arranged to move in prior to the end of the month.

"Which gives us three weekends," Ashley said as they returned home. "I'll have to spend next weekend going through things and make sure Michelle can get over there to get her stuff."

"Give a couple of months notice. That'll give you plenty of time. Just because we can move in, doesn't mean you have to have everything out of your old place by then."

"Oh, good point."

She danced around his apartment.

"I'm so excited. We're getting our own place."

He leaned against the wall and watched her.

"We have our own place here."

She stopped and looked at him.

"Sort of."

"But?"

"But at the new place, there won't be any memories of other girl friends," she said slowly.

He was taken aback.

"You make it sound like I had orgies here or something."

"Did you?"

He shook his head.

"I'm being silly," she said, going to stand by the window to look out. "But after Leslie's visit, I feel like I'm one in a long line. I can't wait to move."

He crossed to stand beside her, unsure of what to say. He couldn't deny Leslie had been here. As had a few other women over the years.

"That's all in the past, sweetheart. If it makes you

unhappy, we can stay at your place until we move."

She leaned against him.

"No, I'll be fine. I'm happy we're moving. You won't have to go any where before that, will you? I don't want to do all this alone."

"I'll make sure I'm here for the move."

6

Tuesday afternoon Ashley almost fell asleep at work. She was so tired. They'd been packing since Sunday afternoon, staying up late to get things organized, then making love before going to sleep.

She had more work than she could handle, but after the praise from her boss, she didn't want to disappoint him by asking to shift some of the load to one of the other accountants.

She got up and walked around, hoping to wake up. Maybe a soft drink with caffeine would help. She couldn't even focus on the numbers.

The phone rang. She lifted it up, still standing. If she didn't get something to wake up, she'd have to close her door and see if a quick catnap would work.

"Ashley Carstairs," she said.

"I like the sound of that," Nick said.

"Me, too. What are you up to? Is something wrong?"

He rarely called her at work.

"Not wrong, just an inconvenience," he said.

She caught on at once.

"Not another trip?"

"Stockholm. But just for a couple of days, I think."

"You said you'd be here for the move."

She panicked. She didn't want to have to do the move alone.

"I will, that's a promise I'll keep. I'm taking one of the new representatives with me. Once I'm sure he'll manage, I'll return home. I probably won't be gone more than two or three days."

She didn't say anything. What was there to say? It was his job. She'd known it from the beginning.

Stockholm.

She looked at the piles of folders, printouts and tax books on her desk. Maybe she should just say goodbye now and take off for Europe with her husband.

She wanted to go so badly she could almost taste it.

"Ashley? I'm sorry."

" Don't be, Nick. I just was wishing I could go with you."

"Ask for time off."

It was so tempting.

"Not now. I can't. But I'll be writing my resignation letter earlier than I thought."

"Good. We'll get settled in our new place and then be ready to go when the next call comes."

"I hope you get another assignment in Paris soon."

"I'll see what I can do."

"You're not leaving before dinner are you?" she asked, suddenly wondering if that's why he called.

"No, we're leaving tomorrow morning. But I thought I'd get over telling you."

"Gee, you make me sound like some kind of grouch or something."

"This way, you'll get your anger out and be loving when we're together tonight."

She laughed.

"You'll be lucky if I stay awake long enough to watch you pack. I'm so sleepy this afternoon."

"We'll go to bed early tonight, I promise."

The conversation went a long way to waking Ashley, and she plunged back into work with renewed enthusiasm. The sooner she finished, the sooner she'd go home.

Michelle called just as Ashley and Nick finished dinner.

"Hi, honey," Ashley greeted her daughter.

"Mom, Charlie's leaving in the morning."

"Oh, so soon? I thought he had a little longer."

"I did, too, but they want him to report to the ship early. You'd think they'd have enough communication specialists they wouldn't need one more right away."

"Is he there with you now?"

"No, he's back at Monterey. We said goodbye earlier. I'm bummed, but there isn't much I can do about it. I guess I needed to whine to someone."

"Whine away, honey. It does seem unfair. But he'll be home in a few months and you two will be getting your own place together like Nick and me."

"You found a place? Oh, tell me about it," Michelle said enthusiastically.

Ashley spent the next few minutes telling her everything about the new apartment, their plans to move and Nick's assignment to Stockholm.

"I thought you were planning to travel with him, Mom. So far you've only been to London. Tell him he can take me if you can't go."

"What about school?" Ashley asked sharply.

"I'm just kidding. Finals are in two weeks. But I'd love to visit Stockholm or Paris or any other exciting locale, come to that."

"I'll let him know. Want to have dinner one night while both our men are away?"

"Sure. Let's go pig out on pizza."

"I'll call you when I see how things go at work tomorrow."

When Ashley hung up, Nick asked about Michelle.

"She's feeling lonely, I think. Charlie's leaving tomorrow."

"She can keep you company while I'm gone," he said.

"We did make a date for pizza. And she said for you to keep her in mind for a junket to Europe when finals are finished."

"The only one I want to go with me is you," he said, reaching for her.

By Thursday, Ashley was convinced she was coming down with something. She plain didn't feel good. And she was so tired, despite getting plenty of rest every night. When Stacy popped into the office at one point, she looked at Ashley with concern.

"Are you all right? You look like something the cat dragged in," she said with her forthright manner.

"What a way to cheer me up. I feel awful, actually. Maybe I should head for home," Ashley said, leaning back in her chair.

She was afraid if she closed her eyes, she wouldn't waken for a month.

"Yeah, well swing by the drugstore on your way," Stacy said.

"Flu medicines you think?"

"Pregnancy test, I think."

Ashley stared at her, her heart racing.

"We use protection."

"The only one hundred percent protection is not doing it at all. And I suspect from seeing that lusty husband of yours that's not the case here. You could be coming down with a cold or the flu, but check it out anyway," Stacy said, taking a stack of completed forms and leaving.

Ashley was rooted to her chair. *She couldn't be pregnant.* She'd had her family–Michelle.

Nick didn't want children or to be tied down. He liked life in the fast lane, liked traveling to a new country every week. He liked sailing in sleek boats and skiing and doing who knew what else.

She couldn't be pregnant. She couldn't go through that again, not at her age, not when she wanted to travel and see the world. They'd talked about moving to London, not discussing all the cares and responsibilities of motherhood.

She wanted a chance to live for herself not another child.

Feeling shocked, she grabbed her purse and headed for home via the drugstore. She had to know. If it was negative, she was worrying for nothing.

But what if the test proved positive?

Trying to keep from panicking until she knew for certain, Ashley hurried through the store and almost flew home. Once there she took the test, holding her breath as she waited for the result.

Positive.

She felt sick.

The last thing in the world she wanted was to start another family.

What would Nick say?

Darrell had been properly receptive to the news she was pregnant and then abandoned her after only a few months of a new baby in the home.

What would Nick do? He told her he didn't want children. They'd planned their future. He was already annoyed with her for the delay in resigning her job.

Another problem. Dare she resign now?

What if she ended up a solo mother again? She'd need the income her job provided. And the security, seniority, stability.

Pacing the small bathroom, Ashley tried to think. But her mind was a jumble of thoughts and she couldn't focus on a single one.

She had to tell Nick. But how?

She'd have to decide what she was going to do. Stay at work? Travel as much as she could before the baby was born? Then what?

Did the new apartment even allow children?

Ashley burst into tears. Her lovely plans for the future had just ended and she didn't know what to do.

For the first time since she met Nick, Ashley didn't want to see him. She hoped his trip proved complicated and urgent and he stayed a month in Stockholm.

Not that the situation would change between now and then, but maybe she'd come up with way to explain how everything they'd planned had changed.

Would he leave? Ask her to leave and keep his bachelor apartment? Would there be other lovely young women parading through in the future like Leslie?

Soaking a wash cloth in cold water, she wrung it out and went to lie down with it over her swollen eyes. A baby should be a joyous event. Instead she was fretting about the future.

She remembered how scared she'd been when she'd found out she was expecting Michelle. She'd been so young at eighteen and had wanted to do so much.

Her second chance had come, and once again, she was pregnant.

There was a knock on the door.

Ashley considered ignoring it. But it sounded again.

"Mom?"

Michelle.

She hadn't even thought of what Michelle might say. Slowly Ashley rose and padded across the apartment in her bare feet. They were supposed to go to pizza tonight. She should have called and postponed.

She opened the door.

"Hi, Mom," Michelle said cheerfully, stopping when she saw her mother. "What's wrong?"

"Come on in."

Ashley felt the tears well again. This was a happy occasion, she had to remember that. She never wanted this new person to feel he or she hadn't been wanted. Even though the timing couldn't have been worse.

"Mom, did you get bad news? Is Nick okay?"

Michelle touched Ashley's shoulder tentatively.

Ashley shut the door, leaning against it for strength.

"Nick's fine, I'm fine. I haven't had bad news just news. Good news," she forced herself to say and tried to smile.

"If this is good news, I don't want bad," Michelle said. "What is it?"

"I'm pregnant," Ashley blurted out and burst into tears again.

Michelle stared at her.

"You can't be," she said, stunned.

Ashley gave a shaky laugh through her tears.

"Thanks, but the pregnancy test says differently."

"Mom, you're too old to be pregnant."

"I am not," Ashley said indignantly.

"Obviously, but I mean, I thought you and Nick planned to travel and do things all over the world, not start a family."

"We do. Did." Ashley pushed away from the door. "Want some tea?" she asked blotting her eyes.

"I don't think tea is going to fix this. Should you be drinking caffeine?"

"One cup of tea isn't going to matter. And I need something."

"When did you find out? How does Nick feel about it?"

"I found out about a half hour ago and Nick doesn't know."

And she was scared to death to tell him. It changed everything. She wondered how long she could go before he'd notice? It'd be the cowardly way, but she wanted his arms around her, she wanted his laughter and his sexy ways to wrap around her and make her feel desirable and wildly exciting.

For the life of her she couldn't envision anything being the same once he knew she was pregnant.

"Wow," was all Michelle had to say.

"I don't want to go out," Ashley said. "Want something here?"

"We can order pizza to be delivered. This is so weird, my mother pregnant. I'm going to have a baby brother or sister. I always wanted one, but not at this late date."

"Well you're getting one now," Ashley snapped.

She'd never known Michelle wished for a sibling. Not that it had been possible with Ashley's cautious attitude around men.

The first time she cut free and let herself live and look what happened.

"Hey, Mom, I think it's great," Michelle said, giving her mother a hug.

Ashley clung. She wanted reassurance. She wanted something to hold on to. What would Nick say? The tears started again.

"Hey, Mom, be happy. Any cravings yet? We could order pizza with pickles and ice cream if you like."

Ashley laughed, hugging Michelle, then stepping away.

"No odd cravings yet. Let's get our regular order."

Nick picked up his bag from the luggage carousel and headed out of customs and toward the long-term parking lot. He was dog tired but anxious to get home. The three day assignment had stretched out to a week. He'd missed Ashley. He'd called her when he could, but with the time differences and their conflicting work schedules, the calls had been few and far between.

And unsatisfactory to boot.

He didn't want to hear her voice, he wanted to hold her, see her enthusiasm when she spotted something new or fascinating. He wanted to hear her laugh, watch her delight in new experiences. Share places he loved, see if she'd love them, too.

As he put his laptop and bag into the car, he made up his mind. He'd force the issue of her resigning if she hadn't already done so.

They'd talked about traveling together, if she was serious, he wanted her with him starting with the next trip or the one after that for sure.

He understood loyalty and admired her for wishing to help the firm through the busiest season, but there was no reason she couldn't give notice now for April sixteenth as her last day. It was only a few weeks away.

He wanted some show of faith in him from his wife. Was she afraid he couldn't support them? Maybe they needed a frank talk about finances.

Aste Technologies had provided billions since the get-go. And continued to do so. He had enough invested to see them secure the rest of their lives. Maybe if she understood that, and being an accountant she'd be able to recognize it at once, she'd feel better about letting go her job.

In the meantime, he'd see if he could keep closer to home, maybe stay in the office for a while and get a better handle on some of the new representatives they'd hired. He wanted to check out their training program to make sure it wasn't lacking in any areas.

The young rep who had gone with him to Stockholm had

been fast and efficient and thrilled to be on his first overseas assignment. But shaky on some of the company's protocols.

After a while travel became routine, as the new rep would find out. Since most of their clients were clustered in a few locations, he'd seen it all before, many times.

Being with Ashley would make it all new again. New and different and far more exciting than he remembered it being in a long time. He wanted to show her the world.

He almost called her from the car, but he'd had enough of telephones. He'd be home in less than half an hour. With no assignment on the horizon, he could focus on packing up his place, helping her with hers and moving into the new apartment that would be their home for the near future.

When Nick opened the door of the apartment a little later, he paused a moment, hearing the soft music, inhaling the tempting aromas coming from the kitchen, catching a whiff of Ashley's special scent. His fatigue fled. He wanted his wife.

"Ashley?"

"Nick?"

She came to the kitchen door, a radiant smile on her face.

"You're home. I'm so happy to see you."

She hurried across the room and flung her arms around him. Her kiss was welcoming, ripe with a hint of things to come. He hugged her closely, delighting in the feel of her slim body, of the fragrance that she always wore. His finger threaded in her silken hair, treasuring the softness.

"I thought you'd call from the airport," she said breathlessly a few moments later.

The pink color in her cheeks caused him to reach up and caress them with his thumbs.

"Phone calls are no substitute for the real thing," he said, kissing her lightly on her lips.

"Dinner will be ready in about twenty minutes. I wasn't sure if your flight would be late or not."

"Uneventful. What's for dinner, it smells good."

"Veal cutlets. Do you like them?"

"I haven't met any meat I don't like."

She laughed, and patted his arm, as if reassuring herself he was here in person.

"And I bet you've tried some I haven't even heard of."

"Not too far off the mark."

"Are you exhausted?" she said as they walked to the kitchen.

"Not too bad. A night's rest will catch me up."

She fussed around preparing the dinner. Nick sat at the counter and watched her, delighting in her femininity. He'd always liked women, some more than others. But none before had given him that deep-down delight that Ashley brought.

"Are you home for a while?" she asked.

"Home for a while. I said I'll be here for the move."

At the comment, she hesitated a moment, looked away.

"That's good."

She concentrated on checking the potatoes in the oven, squeezing them to see if they were done.

"Have you finished packing?" he asked, knowing she and Michelle had been back to their old apartment a couple of times according to their nightly conversations.

"Not finished, but made some headway. There's so much we have to go through. It was easier to keep things than toss them before, but now I don't want to have to move things we no longer need."

She smiled.

"And treasures Michelle thought she'd always want now seem silly. It was fine for her to leave them at her old room, but she, too, doesn't want to bother moving them and finding room in her apartment."

"I imagine she and Charlie will have a simple set up if they plan to move every few years as the military does," Nick said.

"He's going to college once his enlistment is up. They'll only have a couple of moves I think. But it does make sense to streamline."

He took a sip of the coffee she'd prepared him, trying to keep awake. And trying to decipher if there was a change in Ashley. He couldn't put his finger on anything specific, but she seemed to be avoiding his eyes.

She was busy fixing them dinner. She couldn't forever be looking at him. Though Nick admitted he wouldn't mind a little of that wide-eyed, hero-worship look she sometimes gave.

"Did you give your notice?" he asked.

She had her back to him. He could have sworn she tightened up.

"Not yet."

"When, Ashley?" he asked.

He was going to push. He wanted it settled once and for all.

"I told you I can't leave them in the middle of tax season."

"I get that. It's the end of March, the big thrust will be over within a few weeks. No reason you can't give notice for April sixteenth now, is there?"

He didn't imagine the hesitation this time.

"It's complicated," she said.

"No, it's not. Just write up a note saying you quit as of April sixteenth and turn it in."

She said nothing.

Nick felt a spark of anger or frustration.

"Unless you don't plan to do so."

"I want to," she said.

Doubt pierced.

"You want to? What does that mean? I thought we *planned* to. I've been patient, I think, about this. You said you'd quit, that we'd travel. So far I'm traveling and you're not quitting."

Did she want something else? He'd never had a long-term relationship with a woman before. Ashley was so different from the women he'd known, he'd been smitten with her before he knew it.

But they didn't have a long history together. Was this some convoluted way to get something else?

"Let's eat dinner," she said, taking plates down from the cabinet.

"I want an answer."

"I said it's complicated. We can discuss it later if you insist."

"Now."

He didn't like the feeling that swamped him. He rose and crossed the narrow space to stand beside her, turning her to face him.

"What's going on? I thought you liked London. Are you having second thoughts about traveling? Don't want to leave Michelle? What? I have money enough to take care of us, you don't have to worry about that. We can go over our finances later if you want reassurance."

"It's not that. Nick, I know you'll always provide for us. Though I do think I should contribute as well, not be a drain."

"Sweetheart."

He slid his hands under her hair, drawing her closer.

"You'll never be a drain. We'll find something for you to do if you feel you need to contribute. I don't want to make you feel like a dependent. I just want you to be with me. Let's explore everything we can, see the sights most Americans only dream about. We'll go hiking in Nepal, sailing on the Nile, try rock climbing in the Dolomites."

With that, she burst into tears.

Nick was shocked. He stared at her, totally out of his element.

"Ashley?"

He pulled her into his arms, holding her while she cried.

"What's going on?" he asked.

Getting anything out of her was like pulling teeth. Something must be terribly wrong to have her cry like this. She wasn't sick, was she?

Her hands clutched his shirt, he could feel the dampness from her tears soak through. Rubbing her back, he tried to think what he'd said that would bring such a reaction. Had someone she known died rock climbing?

"Ashley?"

"I want to," she said.

Her tears blurred her words.

"I'd love to sail on the Nile, but I got seasick. Only I don't think it was that. And I'd want to hike in Nepal and rock climb but in a few months, I wouldn't be able to get close enough to maintain any balance."

"What are you talking about?"

She clutched his shirt even harder, burying her face against his chest.

"I'm pregnant,' she said.

Nick felt poleaxed.

Ashley was *pregnant?*

Never in his wildest dreams had he pictured himself as a father. They'd used protection. He'd urged her to get birth control pills, but had faithfully donned a condom every time. Every single time.

"How?" he asked, stunned as the implications swept through.

The plans they'd made crumbled.

The life he'd known and loved was changing and there was nothing he could do about it.

"I don't know. Did a condom break? Did we remember every time? Perhaps one of them leaked. Does it matter how?"

She still refused to look at him.

Nick gripped her arms and pushed her back enough to see her face, if she would lift it from gazing at the floor.

"Ashley, look at me," he ordered. "When did you find out? Are you sure?"

She shrugged and looked at him. The miserable expression on her face should have eased his own frustration, but it didn't.

"I took a home pregnancy test last Thursday," she said. "It came up positive."

He let her go and turned to walk into the living room.

He paced the space for a moment, denying this was happening.

He wasn't father material. He hadn't planned on even getting married before he met Ashley. No matter how hard he tried, he couldn't envision himself in a house with a yard and a role in the PTA.

He liked traveling. He liked new environments, new locations, new experiences.

Well this was one heck of a new experience.

"You didn't want a baby, did you?" Ashley asked from the doorway.

He spun around to face her.

"I didn't plan on one, if that's what you are asking. It'll take some getting used to. I never pictured myself as a father."

"I think you'll make a good father."

"Based on what? That I'm male?"

"You're intelligent, honest, honorable."

"I know nothing about children."

"Neither do any parents at the start. Kids don't come with instruction books. We do the best we can."

"It'll take some getting use to," he said.

A whole lot of getting used to.

He thought about his uncle, how he'd never seemed to know how to talk to a kid. How hard it had been to get his point across when telling his uncle something he'd considered important.

How his uncle hadn't been much of a traditionalist or holiday man. Christmases had been austere, birthdays hardly noticed. School plays and sport events missed.

He could be a perfect father if he did everything his uncle had never done.

The buzzer on the kitchen timer sounded.

"Dinner's ready," Ashley said.

Food was the last thing he wanted. But it had been a long time since his last meal. Might as well eat to keep up his strength.

He was going to need it to come to terms with being a father.

"Then, let's eat," he said, heading toward the kitchen, unable to look at Ashley.

Nothing about this homecoming was going as he'd hoped, Nick thought as he ate the delicious meal.

The meat was tender, but could have been cardboard for all he savored it. The potatoes just the way he liked them, only he wasn't interested in enjoying his meal. He was trying to come to terms with the shocking news Ashley had dropped on him.

"When is the baby due?" he asked as the meal ended. Their conversation had been nonexistent.

"I don't know exactly, probably December. Maybe a Christmas baby," she said.

He noticed she had hardly eaten. She was pushing a piece of potato around on her plate.

"Eat up, Ashley, you're eating for two now."

Tears welled as she studied her plate. Blast it, he hadn't wanted her to cry again.

"We'll manage," he said, hoping to end the tears.

"Will kids be allowed at the new apartment?" she asked.

"I have no idea. We'll have to call and check it out. It didn't come up in the discussion as I recall."

"It never came up in any discussion as I recall," Ashley said, standing and tossing her napkin on the table.

She turned and walked quickly into the bedroom.

It had not. There was no denying that.

7

Nick cleared the table and put up the left over food. He stacked the dishes in the sink and filled it with soapy water before heading to the bedroom to talk to his wife. He still felt stunned at the news. At the changes that would come with a baby.

Tired almost beyond belief, he wondered if he could muster his arguments.

What arguments? It was a done deal. They now had to decide how they were going to handle it.

Ashley was in the bathroom when he entered their bedroom. He paced for a few moments, wondering how long she would be. As the minutes stretched out, he wondered what she was doing in there. Maybe he'd just lie down for a few minutes and rest until she came out. It'd been a long day, first getting things set in Stockholm, then the long flight home, then the startling news.

His head hardly touched the pillow before he fell fast to sleep.

Ashley came out of the bathroom dressed in one of her sleep shirts a few minutes later. The bath had helped. She didn't feel as vulnerable as she had earlier. They had to talk, she knew that. She wasn't in the mood for any romantic overtures no matter how much she'd missed Nick over the last few days.

Talk she could handle.

She stopped and stared, feeling chagrined to see him asleep, fully clothed.

Her heart was touched.

He had to be exhausted coming all the way to California from Europe. With the time delays at airports these days, long trips became nightmares of waiting.

She took off his shoes, hesitating over whether to waken him or not, but elected to let him sleep. She took a blanket from the closet and covered him.

Then she checked the rest of the apartment, debating whether to do the dishes or not. Electing not, she flicked off the lights and went to bed. The homecoming had not gone like either of them expected.

Nick awoke to an empty apartment. He lay still a few moments, orienting himself to being back in his own home. Turning, he saw the imprint from Ashley on her pillow. But she wasn't there.

He checked his watch, noting he was still dressed. It was after nine. Ashley had obviously already left for work.

Rising, he headed for the bathroom. He was getting too old to spring back instantly after a fourteen-hour flight and eight time zones. Heck of a thought.

By mid afternoon Nick had tackled the urgent items in his in box and debriefed his trip to the managers involved. He and his partners had shared a quick lunch in Tony's office, then he and Dex had headed back to his own office.

"Need help moving?" Dex asked as they entered Nick's office.

"Might. Still got that pickup truck?"

"Yeah. We can get a couple of the new guys to lend some brawn."

Nick nodded, walking to the window and looking out over the other office buildings in the financial district. The wind must be blowing, he thought idly, watching some trash skip along the gutter of the busy street. People walking were few, but the cars were endless.

"Something on your mind?" Dex asked, leaning against the doorjamb. "You've seemed preoccupied all day. Was there something else we needed to know about the situation in Stockholm or how Davis handled himself?"

Nick shook his head. Slowly he turned and looked at his longtime friend.

"I'm going to be a father."

"What?" Dex was clearly taken aback. "You're kidding."

"Ashley told me last night."

"I thought–" Dex stopped talking.

"Yeah, me, too. I've been nagging her to quit her job so we could travel. Now this. What am I going to do?"

"What do you want to do?" Dex asked cautiously.

"I want to take my wife and fly to Paris, then on to Rome or Hong Kong. Can you picture me changing diapers or attending a Little League game?"

"White picket fence, minivan." Dex chuckled.

"Glad you find it funny," Nick snarled. "Get out, I've got work to do."

"Hey, it's not so bad. Millions of men do it every year."

"I'm not them."

"It can't be all bad, look at Sam Bond."

"Who?"

"Remember him, from college. Sambo? He married right after graduation and he and his wife have three kids."

"You're kidding."

"I kid you not. I get a card from them each Christmas. Her doing, I think. Last year had a picture of the whole family. If he can do it, so can you."

"He doesn't travel like I do. He came from a normal family. He obviously knows what to do about the whole scene."

"So learn, you're reasonably intelligent," Dex said, shrugging his shoulders. "Hey, can I be an uncle?"

Nick glared at him and Dex held out his hands as if warding off a blow.

"Hey, old buddy, I'm happy for you, really I am."

"Go on and get out of here, I have work to do," Nick said, going to sit behind his desk.

He waited until Dex took off, then rose and closed his door. He returned to the window.

He couldn't concentrate on anything. All he could think about was Ashley's announcement last night.

His own childhood had been less than perfect. What did he know about raising a child?

Frustrated, he left work for home. He knew he'd get there before Ashley, but he wanted to be there as soon as she arrived. They had to talk.

Ashley drew on all her professionalism to make it through the day without screaming at the people around her.

She was disappointed at Nick's reaction to her startling

news. It wasn't something she hadn't expected, but secretly she'd hoped that he'd have been a bit more happy about the news.

And the specter of his leaving wouldn't fade.

Her assistant came in toward the end of the day. She shut the door and pulled out a chair near the desk.

"Okay, boss, give. What's wrong?" Stacy asked.

"Nothing."

Ashley looked at her for a moment, wondering where her acting had failed.

"You've asked me twice for folders that are already on your desk. That's never happened before. You're totally out of it and yet you haven't sent the Reams account over to Mr. Popovich for his final approval."

"You were right, Stacy. I'm pregnant."

Ashley threw out the words as if flinging down a gauntlet.

"Wow."

Stacy sat back in the chair and stared at Ashley.

"Won't this put a crimp in Popovich's plans?" Quickly she did the math. "But not for a while. Are you planning to tell him soon?"

Ashley shook her head. She wasn't sure what she was going to do about anything. Especially Nick.

"How are you with this?" Stacy asked.

"What do you mean?"

"Happy, annoyed, blaming that hunk you're married to or what?"

"Happy of course," she said dutifully.

"And is he?"

"He was caught by surprise."

"You, too, I bet. Does this mean he'll stick closer to home now?"

"I don't know. He only got in from Stockholm last night. We didn't have a lot of time to talk before he went to sleep."

Ashley knew she'd deliberately cut off any chance of a conversation, too afraid of what Nick's comments would be.

Sooner or later, they'd have to discuss the situation.

"Are you feeling okay? No problems, right?" Stacy said.

"No, why should there be?"

"Well, no offense boss, but you're not exactly a teeny bopper anymore."

"I'm not that old, either," Ashley said, miffed her young secretary thought she was too old to be having a baby.

Obviously that was not the case.

Would her friends feel the same way?

Michelle had been surprised to find her mother pregnant at this age. How would Allie and Marian view this, she wondered, thinking of two of her closest friends.

None of it mattered. Her husband was the only one she worried about.

Nick was already home when Ashley arrived. She stepped inside the apartment and in only seconds was swept into his arms.

"I've missed you. Today was endless," he said before he kissed her.

She dropped her things to encircle his neck, giving back as much as he gave. Time stopped. Worries ceased. She could only feel the exquisite delight of being with this one man, of losing herself in his touch and soaring above the mundane world to heights only he could lead her to.

When the kiss ended, he lifted her in his arms to carry her to the bedroom.

"Dinner?" she asked breathlessly, almost giddy with joy.

"Later," he said, closing the bedroom door behind him with a quick kick. He set her beside the bed and kissed her again.

"Nick, are you all right with things?" she asked anxiously.

"I'm wide-awake, have had enough sleep and a little while to absorb the news. I'm okay with it. We can talk later, but first, I want to touch you, taste you and make love with you," he said, kissing her as his clever fingers made short work of the buttons holding her blouse in place.

The night was magical, and never gave way to talk.

The next morning both were rushed as they got ready for work. Promising each other to be home early, they said goodbye when Nick dropped Ashley at her office. They still had to discuss things, but this evening was time enough.

For dinner, Nick brought home several cartons of Chinese food. He knew what Ashley liked and didn't want her distracted by cooking and cleaning. They'd eat, rinse the dishes and talk.

She arrived home only moments behind him, a good sign both had arrived early, he thought.

"Oh, Chinese, you're wonderful. I'm starved. Let me change fast and I'll be right out," she said enthusiastically, giving him a warm kiss.

Nick debated following her into the bedroom and decided not. He wanted to give her some perspective on his feelings in the matter and another night of hot love in their bed would not lend itself to discussion.

Time enough for that later, he hoped.

She was back in no time, wearing comfortable jeans and a pullover top in a buttery yellow. Barefoot, she walked across the kitchen and peeked at the food coming from the microwave.

"Smells delicious," she said as she reached up to get plates. In short order they were seated at the small table and eating.

"How are things going at work?" Nick asked, wondering if he dare bring up her quitting at this stage.

His frustration in that regard hadn't diminished with the news of a coming baby. Surely she'd want to quit sooner.

"Hectic."

Ashley glanced at him and smiled, then concentrated on her food.

"How about Aste? I bet Tony and Dex are glad you're back for a while."

"They manage fine without me, but yeah, I think they're glad I'm in town for a while. Watching the new rep in Stockholm gave me some ideas where we need to enhance our training and what's out of date now and can be scrapped."

"Are you in charge of training?"

"No, but I'll review the protocols with Tony and Dex and Josh. Josh is the head of training. He doesn't get into the field enough, I think, to see what's needed. It's mostly theory with him. I should take him on the next assignment."

She was quiet.

He wondered if he should have mentioned another assignment. He wanted her to go with him. This time he wasn't taking no for an answer.

"Dex offered to help us move. He has a pickup truck. And volunteered some brawn from some of the new guys," Nick said, changing the subject. "Or we can hire professionals whichever you want."

She looked at him.

"Did you find out if we can still move to that apartment?"

"I called the manager this morning. There're no restrictions against children. It means the guest room will have to be a nursery, however. We wouldn't have room for Michelle and Charlie when they came to visit."

He watched her swallow, fiddle with her water glass. It was time.

"Ashley, are you sure about this?"

"What do you mean?"

Her eyes met his.

"I'm not going to be a good father. I have no experience in fatherhood or even having a father around. I haven't been around kids since I was one. I'm not cut out for this."

She looked stricken.

"So what do you want me to do about it?"

He shook his head.

"I don't know. You caught me totally unprepared. I haven't a clue where to go from here."

She sat perfectly still, her eyes searching his, looking for what?

"Nobody has experience being a parent until they are one," she said slowly.

"But most people have experiences being a kid of a parent. Uncle Henry raised me. And if he's the best parent around, the world's in trouble."

"You mentioned him before when you told me your parents were dead. Still, he was a relative and took you in. He must have done something right, you're a terrific man."

Nick shrugged. He believed anything he'd accomplished had been his own doing, not as a result of Henry's parenting skills or lack of them.

"Henry was a bachelor first and foremost. My mother's parents didn't want the responsibility of raising a child after her death. My dad's parents were divorced, his father lived on the East Coast and didn't step in. His mother was remarried to a man—"

Nick stopped suddenly. She'd remarried a man who traveled a lot in his line of work and she didn't want to stay home with her grandson and miss all the travel.

He'd been resentful as a child.

Yet he wanted the same thing for Ashley. He wanted her to travel with him and not stay home and watch some baby he hadn't ever planned for.

"Who didn't want children?" Ashley prompted.

"Something like that. You have to see I wouldn't be a good role model for any kid."

"Well this isn't something we can say, sorry, not for us, and return to the store or something," she said with some heat. "I'm not exactly dancing for joy at this turn of events. I thought I'd raised my family. But it happened. And I feel sorry for a baby that neither parents particularly wants."

She tossed her napkin down and dashed from the table, running into the bedroom and slamming the door behind her.

Nick heard her crying but he was unable to move.

What a legacy for a child.

The whole situation took some getting used to. She was right, there was no sending it back.

For the rest of his life, he was going to be a father.

And he'd never, ever, not even for one second, let this child think he wasn't wanted.

Nick knew first-hand how hard that was to deal with.

Ashley couldn't stop the tears. He'd all but said she had to do something about the baby. But what?

She'd had longer to get used to the idea of the baby. She could feel the subtle changes in her body, foretelling major changes to come. One day she'd hold her son or daughter in her arms. Rock it, nurse it, love it.

Would the baby's father be anywhere around?

Or would Nick have cut out long before then, convinced he'd make a bad father?

And too caught up in his fast lane life to stop long enough to visit his child?

She heard the home phone ring, but didn't move. Nick was home, he could answer it.

Slowly the tears ceased. She lay exhausted, unable to get up, unable to move. She should go wash her face or something, but lethargy won. She closed her eyes, not falling asleep, just too tired and dispirited to move.

Nick knocked on the door and the sound tore at her heart. This was his home, his bedroom, he didn't need to knock.

"Yes?"

He opened the door a crack and peered in, the phone in one hand.

"Tony and Dex are planning an impromptu sail this weekend. The weather is supposed to be perfect. We're invited."

The mere thought of the wide Bay and the bobbing boat almost made her sick.

"I can't go," she said quickly. "Michelle and I are packing tomorrow. Why don't you go, though. It'll be fun for you to be with your friends."

He hesitated a moment.

"Are you sure?"

"Yes, I'm sure,' she said, keeping her eyes closed.

It was dumb, but now that she had said it, she wished the words back. She didn't want him to go off on fun-filled adventures without her.

She wanted him to say, no, I wouldn't have fun without my wife.

"Okay, then," Nick said.

He spoke into the phone again.

"Ashley can't make it. But I can. What time?"

He moved away, still talking.

She felt a flare of anger that was totally irrational. She'd told him to go. He was taking her at her word. Why did it make her angry?

Because she wanted to be the center of his universe, she realized. As he'd become the center of hers.

Tears welled again, but she damped them down. Rising, she headed for the bathroom.

Joining Nick in a few minutes, face bathed and makeup donned, she smiled, hoping she could carry this off. He was sitting on the sofa, the TV playing softly.

"So when are you going tomorrow?" she asked.

"We're leaving at eight. When are you and Michelle getting together?"

He patted the cushion beside him, indicating he wanted her to join him.

"Not until ten. Will you be home for dinner?"

Ashley sat beside him, hoping he'd pull her into his arms.

As if he read her mind, he put his arm around her shoulders and drew her close.

"Yes, I'll be home around four or so. Will you feel like cooking or shall I pick up something?"

"I'll put on a stew that can cook all day while we work. Can we eat at my place? That way I can watch the stew during the day and won't have to get it over here."

"I can be at your *former* apartment whenever you say," he replied.

Ashley smiled, remembering how insistent he was she think of his apartment as home. Maybe with the new one.

If he stayed.

"What are you watching?" she asked.

"Travel channel. They're showing a segment on the world's best beaches."

Figured, even at home, he was longing for distant shores. Ashley snuggled down beside him, watching as the exotic scenes played on the screen.

She longed for them, as well. How could she fault Nick for being honest?

She couldn't fault him for anything. She loved him. He hadn't change a bit since she'd met him. He was wildly sexy, exciting, dynamic. He seemed to like spending time with her, though she didn't think she offered as much as someone like that blond bombshell who had showed up. Yet he was satisfied, happy.

Or was he? They'd made such wonderful plans before they married. And so little had come about.

Due to her.

She should have quit her job. But if he left, where would she be without work?

Maybe there was more she could do to live up to the plans they'd made, the ones she'd been as excited about as he. She doubted Mr. Popovich would fire her if she took another week off. She had loads of vacation time on the books.

She could become the perfect wife, doing everything he wanted, so he'd never wish to leave. And she wouldn't harp on the baby nor bring the subject up more than she needed to in the normal course of events.

Once the baby was born, he'd see he'd be a great father. She hoped he'd be willing to try.

What caused a man to leave a family? She'd never understood Darrell's defection. And once he left, he never contacted her, never saw Michelle after she was three months old. The divorce had been handled through attorneys. He'd left the state and never paid child support even though it had been part of the settlement.

How would she handle things if Nick left? How would she handle her life if he left?

Fear clutched her heart.

She wouldn't be able to, she thought. In the short time they'd been together, he'd become an integral part of her being. The plans they'd made wouldn't come about now or at least for another eighteen years. Would Nick be patient that long?

"We should have a housewarming party when we get the new apartment," she said.

He looked at her.

"What brought that up?"

"The luau."

She gestured to the scene on the television.

"Reminded me of our move and new place. Don't you want friends to see it? I do. I'm excited about it."

"Whatever. It's just another apartment."

She smiled and patted his knee.

"Maybe it's a girl thing."

"Like nesting. Are we getting a lot of new furniture as well?"

"Not a lot."

Mostly baby stuff eventually, but she didn't voice that.

"I like this sofa and the chairs I have in my *former* apartment will blend in. We can decide before moving furniture if we're not taking everything."

She'd be agreeable, fun to be around. And they'd build such wonderful memories he'd never want to leave her.

Saturday proved difficult sorting through her past with Michelle. Ashley had several boxes and bags for the trash or charity waiting by the door by the time Nick arrived for dinner. She and Michelle had packed up most of the books and pictures and all the kitchen things.

Ashley wanted to go through Nick's kitchen before giving up any of her pots and baking pans. She suspected she'd want to keep most since his place seemed light on cookware.

Ashley kept to her vow to be the best of companions. She kept the conversation light at dinner.

Michelle seemed to pick up on her mood and contributed funny anecdotes from college.

Nick regaled them with the snafus he'd encountered in early trips and the sailing trip that day.

The time passed quickly and with all the fun Ashley hoped for. She was pleased with her strategy.

Before they left to return to Nick's place, he walked through the apartment.

"We'll get some professionals in to pack up the rest. You need to conserve your energy," he said.

"I'm fine."

"Maybe. But tomorrow, we'll stay home and rest."

She smiled in anticipation. The last time they'd stayed home to rest, they spent most of the day in bed but not at all in restful pursuits.

However Nick meant exactly what he said. Sunday he brought her breakfast in bed and left her to eat it, saying he had the paper to read.

When Ashley got up and dressed, he urged her to sit on the sofa to read or watch television. She didn't wish to do either.

"I want to spend time with you," she said, leaning over him at the dining table and looking at the crossword puzzle he worked.

"I'm here. I can watch a movie on TV if you like."

"Anything special you want to see?"

What was going on?

"No, what would you like?"

"I'd like to go for a walk. It's gorgeous outside. April is a lovely month in San Francisco, before the fog makes its daily appearance. Let's go to Golden Gate Park and visit the Tea Gardens," she suggested.

"Sure you don't want to rest up? You've been working hard lately. With the baby and all, I thought you should rest."

Michelle had asked Ashley privately before they'd left last night if Nick knew about the baby. No mention had been made all evening. Ashley assured her he knew.

This was the first time he'd voluntarily mentioned it.

And she didn't like it at all.

She wasn't an invalid. She wanted to do something fun with her husband.

"I'm getting plenty of rest," she said evenly.

"So no nap needed?" he asked.

She remembered other days when they had napped. Slowly she began to smile. Maybe she'd forego the park and spend the afternoon in Nick's arms instead.

8

The next few days sped by. Ashley didn't bring up the subject of the baby around Nick. He never mentioned it either. It was as if there was a huge elephant in the living room that neither admitted to. How long would it last?

The strain was starting to tell. She accepted the fact of the new child and was growing excited. She wanted to talk about the baby, make plans, decide on names, look at furniture, buy a new teddy bear. The list was endless.

But she tiptoed around Nick. They talked about work or about the move. Even the talk of travel had ended. Had he given up on her?

Fear clutched her every time she thought about the future.

Wednesday afternoon, Nick called. Ashley knew as soon as she recognized his voice that he had another trip lined up. He was calling to alert her.

"What's up? Are you bringing home dinner?"

"I can. What do you want?"

" Barbecue sounds good."

"I'll take care of it. I have a trip tomorrow. A short one, but I'm needed."

"Where to?" She caught her breath. "How short?"

"Las Vegas. One of our security setups at a casino seems to have a glitch. Can't tell for sure if it's a problem or lack of training for the security people. I won't be gone long. A day or two at the most."

"I've always wanted to go to Las Vegas," she said slowly.

"So come with me."

"Okay, I will," she said, startling them both.

"You will?" he repeated. "I leave in the morning, won't be home before Friday night if then."

"Or we could stay over the weekend and see a couple of shows. Even go swimming. Isn't it always hot in Vegas?"

"I'll make the reservations. See you at dinner."

He hung up before she could say another word. Probably thinking she'd change her mind.

Ashley replaced the receiver and drew a breath. She was committed.

What would Mr. Popovich say? He was likely to kick up a fuss, but so what? She had time due her and a day or two wouldn't break the firm. She'd take work with her if she could, but the firm preferred to keep the client's records on the premises.

Still, if needed she could make it up next week by working later each day. She'd been leaving at five every day Nick was home. Next week she'd stay as late as needed. It was only a week until tax day. She'd make sure all her work was finished the day before. Who could argue with that?

For this weekend, however, she was going to spend every moment she could with her husband, seeing the fabulous side of Las Vegas.

The weekend in Las Vegas was all Ashley hoped traveling with Nick would be. They swam in the luxurious pool at one of the largest of the magnificent hotels on the Strip where they were staying. They saw two shows, ate decadently and made love in the sumptuous king-size bed.

For four days Ashley put reality away and enjoyed the life she'd so hoped to have embarked on when she and Nick married. It was fabulous.

But reality returned Monday when she had to return to work.

"I'll be late tonight," she said as Nick prepared to drop her off at her office.

"How late?"

"Pretty late. Don't wait up."

He caught her arm as she started to get out of the car.

"What do you mean don't wait up? You can't work that late. Six or seven maybe, but not later."

"I have a lot of work to get through. Taking two days off last week means I have to get it done by working later to get caught up."

"What, are you planning to make up the sixteen hours you missed by working them through after normal business hours? Four hours a night?"

"If I have to. I told Mr. Popovich I'd get the work done and Friday's the deadline."

"I don't want you working so late. You need to rest."

"I need to live up to my word and have the work completed on time. The clients are depending on us. On me. I won't let them down."

"You need to rest," he repeated.

"I appreciate your concern, but Nick, I do know how to run my life. It's only for a few days."

"What about me?" he asked.

"I'll see you when I get home," she said, tugging her arm free and getting out of the car.

Some way to make herself indispensable to her husband, she thought guiltily, virtually ignoring him while she plunged into work. But it was only until Friday. She'd be caught up then and could spend more time with him.

She could take a leave of absence for a few months. To see what they could have had if the baby had not come along?

Wouldn't that make staying home that much harder in the long run, she questioned as she hurried to her office.

She yearned to explore different cities, visit places she'd only dreamed about. Or even enjoy mundane things like sleeping in if she wished or staying up late. Or shopping on Wednesdays when the stores weren't crowded, instead of always on the weekend when half of the city was also shopping.

Arriving at her desk, she quickly set to work. The sooner she got started, the sooner done.

Ashley was tired when she unlocked the door to the apartment. It was after ten. Nick opened the door and drew her into his arms. His kiss was sweet. She couldn't have handled much more.

"Did you eat any dinner?" he asked, as she took off her coat.

"Yes." No need to tell him it was a sandwich and chips.

"Time for bed, then," he said ushering her into the bedroom.

In less than ten minutes Ashley was in bed, and asleep in less than two more.

The pattern repeated itself every day until Thursday. At last she was finished. Glowing with a sense of accomplishment, Ashley sent the last form off for signing. She'd beat the deadline by twenty-four hours.

She was bone-tired and almost groggy with want of sleep, but she'd done it. Tomorrow would be a piece of cake and then she'd have the weekend free of worries.

Next week she'd approach Mr. Popovich about cutting back her hours or that leave of absence.

She called Nick at work, wanting to let him know she'd be home before dinner tonight.

"He's not here," his secretary said.

"Oh, will he be back before closing?" she asked.

"I don't believe so. Can I take a message?" the woman asked.

"It's his wife. I'll catch him at home later."

She wondered where he'd gone. He hadn't said anything about going anywhere, had he? They'd barely spoken over the last few days.

She collapsed into bed the minute she reached home. He drove her to work every day, and insisted she take a cab home each night. Otherwise, their conversation had been decidedly lacking in any hint of intimacy.

The restraints of tax season were over. She could do more with her own life now, make sure she was the kind of wife he wanted to stay with.

Nick wasn't Darrell. She had to remember that.

But Nick wasn't Nick, either, Ashley thought Saturday afternoon. He seemed distant. No other way to describe it.

He'd been happy enough when she arrived home early on

Friday, but beyond commenting he was glad she was cutting back her hours to a more normal routine, he'd said little.

"Want to do some packing?" she asked.

He'd looked up from the paper he was reading and shook his head. "Time enough." He looked down again.

Studying him for a moment, Ashley knew he wasn't reading. His eyes almost bore a hole in the paper, but they weren't moving.

"Something wrong?"

He shook his head.

She didn't want to do chores. She was free from the exacting workload that characterized tax deadlines. She wanted to do something frivolous and fun.

But now that she was ready, Nick seemed not to care.

"We could go do something."

He folded the paper and tossed it on the coffee table.

"Like what?"

"I don't know. What would you like to do?"

"We could go to the movies, I guess."

Ashley wrinkled her nose. She didn't like that idea at all.

"Sitting in the dark watching someone else act isn't my idea of fun today," she said.

"What is? I thought you'd be tired and want to rest up."

She wasn't sure if that was a comment about her pregnancy or her work, both of which were touchy subjects.

"Well, I don't. Let's do something fun."

Just then the home phone rang.

Nick picked it up.

Ashley rose and went to the window and looked out over the Bay. It shouldn't be as hard as this to get him interested in doing something with her.

A niggling fear settled in her stomach. He was distancing himself. If nothing else, he should have suggested they spend the day in bed, as they had on their honeymoon. It wasn't that long ago.

Yet it was, a lifetime ago.

Before the baby.

She sighed softly, tears threatening. Was she going to lose him because of their baby? It wasn't like she'd deliberately set out to get pregnant.

This changed all her hopes for the future, too, didn't he realize.

"Ashley."

She turned around to look at him.

"Annie and Tony are throwing an impromptu barbecue today and want us to join them. Are you up to it?"

She nodded. At least it'd get them out of the apartment.

Tony's place was in an older neighborhood out near the ocean. They had a huge old home that had been built after the great 1906 earthquake and had been in his family for generations. The yard was guarded by a high wooden fence, the patio at the back of the house shaded by a trellis with a wisteria starting to bud.

Ashley met Tony and his wife at the wedding. She greeted him and Annie. Tony and Nick were close and Ashley wanted to do what she could to cement relations with him and his wife.

There were several couples already in the yard. She recognized Dex, leaning near a young woman flirting like crazy. She smiled at Nick, wanting to share the moment, but he was already talking with Tony in low tones.

"You two aren't working, are you?" she asked suspiciously.

"Only catching up on a couple of things," Nick said.

"That's their favorite theme," Annie said, laughing. "Come and meet my sister and leave them to their shop talk."

She nodded toward a pretty woman in a wheelchair.

"What can I get you to drink first?" Tony asked.

"A non-caffeinated soft drink," Nick said, putting his arm around Ashley's shoulders.

"Right, the mother-to-be, Tony replied.

He smiled at Annie, then reached over the bar and pulled out a 7-UP for Ashley.

"Nick, glad you could make it," a blonde of about twenty-five walked by, smiling at Nick, and nodding politely at Ashley.

"Melody," he said with a nod of acknowledgment.

"Here you go," Tony said, handing Ashley a tall glass.

"Is everyone here from work?" she asked taking a sip.

Tony handed another drink to Nick and glanced around.

"Pretty much. A couple of the neighbors, but most are from Aste. Introduce her around, Annie."

"I intend to. See to it you two don't talk shop all afternoon. Come on, Ashley, let's go see Julia before someone else arrives I have to greet. Are you totally thrilled about the baby?"

"Sure," Ashley said, trying to smile.

It was the standard response.

Annie looked around and then leaned close.

"We're expecting, too. Tony didn't want to tell anyone yet, but I thought another mother-to-be would want to know."

"How wonderful. Your first?"

Annie nodded.

"Only Julia knows. We plan to tell folks soon, but for now, it's just family and very close friends."

Ashley wondered later if it had been a mistake to come.

Everyone knew Nick. They greeted him warmly, exchanging insider jokes and comments. When introduced to Ashley everyone was polite, but she imagined she could hear the question tumbling in their minds—what had he seen in her?

Despite the informality of the barbecue, the talk inevitably turned to business. Ashley felt more and more left out as even the pretty, young women seemed to have a vested interest in the computer aspects or the security planning.

After chatting with Julia, she wandered around the yard, noticing how meticulously it was kept. For a moment, she tried to visualize Nick with a rake in hand. The image wouldn't come.

She glanced at Dex, still flirting with that pretty woman. She couldn't picture him married.

When she looked at Nick she tried very hard to see him in a yard pushing a little child on a swing. Neither the child nor Nick would appear.

"I'm Margot," a young woman said coming to stand beside Ashley. "Annie sent me over. I'm pregnant, too. It's my second, but I'm just as thrilled as I was the first time."

Ashley smiled.

"It's my second, too. But there'll be twenty years between my babies."

"Oh, wow, that's like starting completely over. How cool for Nick to be able to have a family. He's been such a lone wolf. I never thought he'd settle down. Have you picked out names yet?"

Ashley shook her head, "You?"

Margot was off and running. She and her husband had a list of names and were thinking about giving the child several, not just a first and second. She then talked about her son, age two, her husband Brian who was over there somewhere. She motioned vaguely with her hand, never taking her attention from Ashley.

"He loves these kinds of things. I'd rather stay home with Jimmy. Want to find chairs somewhere? I'm ready to sit."

Ashley agreed, glad someone at the party seemed happy she was there.

The afternoon passed pleasantly with Margot. Ashley enjoyed her company especially since her husband seemed content to be in discussion groups from the office. The laughter that rang out from time to time made Ashley wistfully wish he'd included her, but she was enjoying Margot's company.

Annie came by with her sister at one point and their discussion was lively and fun. Margot also knew the secret. Discussing babies proved to be better this time around, Ashley thought. Her own excitement began to grow while exchanging hopes and plans with others in the same situation.

The food, when served around seven, was delicious. Tony commandeered several of the men to help with the meat. The salads and side dishes appeared as if by magic from the kitchen.

"For an impromptu affair," Ashley commented to Margot, " Annie and Tony sure have everything organized."

"Tony's the organized one of the group. Nick's the computer guru and Dex is best at body guarding," Annie said. "They play to their strengths."

"Dex is a bodyguard?"

She looked at the man with the shaggy hair, trying to picture him in a tense situation, and failing. He looked too much like a boy-next-door type.

"Oh, he does other things, planning security, training in self-defense, defensive driving, and all. But yeah, he's their head for personal security."

"What area does your husband work in?" Ashley asked Margot, looking around for Nick.

He was talking to the same blonde Dex had been talking with earlier.

"He works with Nick in computers. But he doesn't know as much, nor can he gain the customers' confidence as quickly as Nick can. It helps that he speaks several languages, though most of the international computer work they do is done in machine language."

They ate buffet style. Nick and Tony stood near the grill, keeping an eye on the second round of steaks while they ate. Some of the others gravitated toward them.

Ashley met Margot's husband then excused herself to join her husband.

"Hey," Nick said when she stepped up beside him. "Enjoying yourself?"

She nodded, holding up her plate.

"The food is delicious."

"Some of us were talking about taking a sail tomorrow," Tony said. "You and Nick plan to join us. The forecast's for good winds and warmer temperatures."

"I don't think so," Ashley said, remembering their sail a few weeks earlier. "But I'm sure Nick will be up for it."

"Might take you up on it," he murmured.

Not the answer Ashley wanted. She kept her smile in place, however, not letting the disappointment show.

She wanted him to stay with her on Sunday. This was their first time together in a while and separate plans for Sunday wasn't what she expected.

Early Sunday Ashley awoke to find Nick all ready dressed. He suggested she take the day to rest up after her hectic week. He was off to sail with Tony and Dex. She watched as he left, with barely a kiss on her cheek.

By mid morning, Ashley had rested all she wanted. She left a note telling Nick she'd gone to her apartment, then headed out to continue the sorting she'd begun. They were due to move soon. Somehow she hoped by leaving everything in her past behind, Nick would have to stay.

Would giving up her apartment be foolish? Or a way to cement their relationship even more so they would have to face the challenges ahead together?

She knew he'd lined up some friends from work to help with the actual transportation of their furniture and boxes, but she needed to sort through a few more areas to make sure she only took things she wanted.

When Ashley reached the apartment, she called Michelle. "I'm at the apartment packing, want to come over?"

"I'd love to, Mom. I've been studying until I'm almost brain-dead. My finals are this week and I need a break before plunging back in," she replied.

"We could do something fun if you'd rather. Seems a

shame for you to take a break and then end up working," Ashley said.

She was trying not to think of Nick spending the day away from her. She missed him. What if this was the beginning of a pattern?

Or the beginning of the end?

"I don't mind. I'll be there soon. Is Nick helping?"

"No, he's sailing with friends again."

Ashley wondered if she should confide her doubts to her daughter. Michelle was grown now. Ashley didn't need to shelter her any longer.

Yet old habits died hard. She didn't want Michelle to worry about her and Nick. They'd be fine.

She hoped.

Once off the phone, she tried to run from her thoughts as she began pulling down the dishes from the cupboards. Some she'd donate to charity, a couple of special pieces she'd take with her.

Michelle breezed in a little while later. Ashley had sorted most of the food still in the cupboards, boxing the spices and condiments, and putting the rest in bags to take home with her.

"Look what I got," Michelle said, giving her mother a hug. "Fresh bagels from Manny's. Poppyseed for you, onion for me, plus lox and cream cheese."

"That sounds great. I'm hungry."

"Well, you are eating for two, Michelle said.

She cleared a space at the small table and placed the bag on it. The aroma wafted in the air.

"My mouth was watering all the way here. You're lucky I

didn't stop to eat mine on the way," she said cheerfully as she looked around for plates. "Where is everything? Are we boxing it all up today?"

"Only the things I want to give away. You can have first crack at anything you want. Nick has a set of dishes we're using. Now that we're married, we'll get what we want as a couple."

She stared at the dishes, remembering Nick telling her to get what she wanted, that he didn't care that much.

She wanted Nick to be as excited about setting up house together as she was.

"Who did Nick go sailing with?" Michelle asked as they sat at the table as they had for so many years.

"He and his friends from work, Dex and Tony. It's Tony's boat."

"The sailboat you went on?" Michelle asked.

Ashley nodded, slathering cream cheese on her bagel and then placing some of the fish on top. Biting into it, she savored the delightful flavors.

"Guys only?" Michelle asked before taking a bit of her own.

"I don't think so," Ashley said, "I was invited, but declined. I don't need to feel seasick, I get enough queasiness from the baby as it is."

Dex's words suddenly echoed in her mind–playboy of the western world. Surely Nick would honor their marriage vows. He wasn't flirting with other women. They were happy.

Or they were until she got pregnant.

"Mom? Are you all right? You have the most peculiar expression on your face," Michelle said, looking at her in concern.

"I'm fine. Just thinking."

Thinking about the desolation she'd face if Nick decided marriage wasn't what he wanted. Especially one that now included a baby.

"I changed my mind," Michelle said. "Let's finish lunch, and then go out. It's a beautiful day, not too hot, and with a steady breeze. We can go to Golden Gate Park, walk around, go to the arboretum or something. What do you say?"

Ashley looked around at the mess on the counters and floor.

Golden Gate Park was where she'd wanted to go with Nick. However, she'd take what she could get.

"Sounds good to me. We'll leave this until next weekend."

"Or just leave it all behind. Start your new life with all new things," Michelle suggested.

Nick leaned back, closing his eyes and shutting out the sounds of his friends talking. He let the wind whip through his hair as he absorbed the warmth from the sun.

This was what he loved. If he had ever been able to figure out a way to make a good living from sailing, he'd have done that for his career. But the only ways he'd explored consisted of chartering the boat, offering fishing tours or something that would have strangers in his personal space.

Better to do the job he was so suited for and splurge on Tony's boat when he got the chance.

And the chances were likely to become fewer and fewer.

He shook his head.

He couldn't get past the fact he was going to become a father.

Technically, maybe he was already considered one or a step-father for sure. But at least Michelle could stand on her own feet. What did he know about babies?

He knew enough that most men who had children didn't take off sailing on a whim. Didn't plan to extend work trips by a few days to explore the neighboring towns and cities. He wasn't even sure he knew any men with children who went rock climbing or scuba diving.

Some of the men at work had families. They also had homes that took a lot of work.

Tied down for eighteen years. Could he do it?

"Hey, man, come take a turn at the helm," Tony called.

Nick opened his eyes. Might as well enjoy the day while he could.

"What are you going to do?" he asked as he ambled over and replaced Tony at the wheel.

"Catch some rays. Talk with that pretty lady I brought."

He winked at Annie.

"Fine. I'm heading out beyond the bridge," Nick said, nodding toward the Golden Gate Bridge that spanned the opening to the San Francisco Bay from the Pacific.

"Go for it. The weather's great, the swells won't be too big."

Tony went to sit beside his wife.

Dex and his date were forward, enjoying the bow.

Josh Pendar was the other man from work. He and his steady were lounging on the aft section.

Nick wished he'd stayed home or brought Ashley. But he didn't think she'd be up to another sail until after the baby came. She hadn't fared so well on the one they took.

Who suspected then that she was pregnant?

Still, the return trip had been fun. He entertained some thought to buying a boat for the two of them. He could take some time from work. They could have sailed to Hawaii or Alaska or something.

Unless they moved to London. Funny how they hadn't discussed that at all once he'd learned about the baby.

He studied the water ahead of them, turned into the wind a bit more, calling for Josh and Tony to trim the sails to capture the full thrust of the wind. Sailing usually completely drove any problems from his mind. It refreshed him.

Not today, however.

He kept thinking of the future, wondering what he was going to do. He and Ashley hadn't known each other for long. He'd thought they'd marry and things would continue much as before for him only he'd have his wife with him when he visited other cities and countries.

The reality so far had proved far different. And was changing even more with a baby on the way.

"Hey, man, you still need us to help move your furniture in a couple of weeks?" Dex asked.

"Hold off on plans," Nick said. "I'm not sure I'm signing the lease."

9

Ashley and Michelle enjoyed the afternoon in Golden Gate Park. They wandered the paths in the oasis of green surrounded by apartments and houses on three sides, and the Pacific on one end.

The Japanese Tea Gardens were lovely and quiet. They savored the ritualistic Japanese Tea Ceremony and browsed the gift shop before heading to the Conservatory of Flowers. Examining the exotic varieties of flowers and plants was fascinating, but Ashley loved the butterfly exhibit best. Would her baby like to watch the small insects flutter around?

As the afternoon wore on, she grew tired. But she was determined to make the most of her day off as Nick was his.

"Want to eat dinner at the Wharf?" she asked Michelle.

Her daughter's favorite treat when growing up was to indulge in clam chowder at one of the hole-in-the-wall restaurants at the Wharf. Not the fancy ones flooded by tourists, but one of the smaller places that catered to locals.

"I'd love it. Why not call Nick and tell him where to join us." Michelle suggested.

"Good idea. I'm not sure when they were due back. Depends on how far they went, I guess."

When she dialed his cell phone he was out of service range. She called the apartment and left a message, explaining carefully where the restaurant was so he could find it.

"I don't know if he'll make it," she said slowly when she hung up.

"It's weird, isn't it?" Michelle said as they began slowly walking toward the Muni bus stop.

The metro line would take them to downtown where they could catch the Powell Street cable car which would take them to the wharf. From there, they could walk back to Nick's place after dinner.

"What is?" Ashley asked.

"Being married. For you and for me."

"It's sure changed things," Ashley agreed.

"Not so much for me as for you. Charlie's hardly here. We spent less time together than I expected. Did I tell you he's now talking about continuing in the Navy? He mentioned it a couple of times when he was here. Yesterday on the phone he said he is really thinking about it. He likes that kind of life. But I don't know if I will."

"You'd get to travel."

"Maybe. But he'd have to be on sea duty some of the time—gone for months. I'd be stuck somewhere in the States where he was last stationed. It's a dangerous profession these days. He has the chance to get out in another year, why wouldn't he?"

"You two need to discuss it. Surely he wouldn't make a decision like that without discussing it with you," Ashley said.

"Who knows? I sometimes feel I don't know him as well as I thought I did. He's changed since we were in high school together."

"So have you. You know what you want to do and are

working toward a degree to enable you to teach. You can do that anywhere so moving wouldn't be a hardship. I'm sure he's changed since being in the Navy."

"Mom, you're the one who longs for new places and new sights. I like living here. I don't want to pack up and move every few years. I sort of pictured us living here in San Francisco all the time. Like his parents do."

"Tell Charlie. He needs to know how you feel," Ashley said, struck by her own words.

Maybe she needed to share her fears and concerns with Nick.

But to what end? To have him confirm them?

The phone rang four times before it switched over to voice mail. Where was she, or had she forgotten to charge her phone again?

"Ashley? It's Nick. I'm at Tony's. The sailing was great. We just got back and are having dinner in a little while. Call me when you get home and I'll come get you."

He rattled off Tony's phone number and hung up.

He tried the phone at her apartment and got no response there either. Maybe she was between the two and would call back in a few minutes.

"Ashley coming?" Tony asked when Nick rejoined the others in the great room.

"She didn't answer. I'll try again in a bit."

He tried twice more before dinner, leaving a brief message each time. He was starting to worry. It was already dark outside, she wouldn't have stayed out so late if she'd gone for a walk or something. Where was she?

As soon as he finished eating, he left.

He wasn't worried precisely, Ashley was grown and had taken care of herself for many years before meeting him. But he was concerned. Where was she?

"That was fun, Mom. Call me next time you want to pack up," Michelle teased as she stopped at the bus stop.

The next bus would take her all the way out to the university, near her apartment. A short walk and she'd be home.

"Next time we really have to pack up. We're due to move soon. We can't keep stalling," Ashley said.

The big bus pulled into the curb.

"Gotta go. Love ya."

Michelle gave her mother a quick hug and stepped onto the bus.

It was only a few blocks to home. Ashley turned and headed for the apartment. She'd done too much. She was so tired all she wanted to do was go to bed.

But it had been fun to spend the day with Michelle. They didn't do it often enough.

She knew her daughter had her own life now. And she had Nick. But for so many years it had been the two of them against the world.

"You need to keep your phone charged," Nick said as soon as she opened the apartment door.

"What?"

"I called you several times," he said from across the room. "Since you never called back I can only assume you didn't get the voice mail. And when I got home, I heard your message. If you'd been able to take my call, we could have hooked up for dinner."

"I'm sorry you missed dinner with us," she said, taking off her jacket.

Was he angry? He seemed distant.

"You missed dinner with us at Tony's. We went there after sailing," he said.

"Did you enjoy the sailing?" she asked.

He shrugged. "It was all right. Would have been better if you'd been there."

A warm glow spread through Ashley. She smiled.

"I was afraid I'd get sick again. It wasn't that great when it was the two of us. I didn't want to be sick among a boat load of good sailors."

"How's Michelle?" he asked.

"Fine. We started to pack some things at the other place, but decided to spend the day at the park instead. Then we ate at the Wharf. She has finals this week and wanted a break from studying."

"I heard your message when I got in. You could have tried my cell."

"When I did, you were out of range."

"You look tired," he said, studying her.

"I am. I thought I'd take a quick shower and head for bed."

She might have been talking to a neighbor for all the closeness she felt with this conversation. Why didn't he come across the room and kiss her?

"I'll stay up a bit longer. Good night," Nick said, turning toward the computer he kept in the alcove.

Ashley tried to ignore the hurt she felt, but it was impossible.

"Nick, we need to talk."

She'd advised her daughter of the same thing. It was time she took her own advice.

"Not tonight," he said.

"Soon, then."

He nodded.

Nick drove her to work the next morning, kissing her deeply before letting her out of the car.

"See you tonight," he said.

Ashley felt better than she had in a few days after that kiss. She planned to discuss a leave-of-absence with her boss before telling Nick. If things went as she planned, she could tell him at dinner.

It was spring in many parts of the world. She'd love to return to England or visit another country in Europe if Nick got an assignment there.

Mr. Popovich wasn't happy with her request. He threatened to terminate her employment entirely. Despite the fear of that very thing, Ashley held firm.

She hadn't told her boss she was pregnant and didn't think her assistant has spread the news, so she was spared any discussion about what she was going to do long-term when he reluctantly granted her request.

With the promise of time off beginning at the end of the month, Ashley returned to her office. She'd check in with the landlord of the new apartment next, once she cleared the crucial work from her desk, to see if she could start moving things in early.

Caught up in the client files awaiting her review, Ashley didn't realize how much of the morning had passed until she picked up the phone when it rang at eleven-thirty.

"Ashley, I've got to go to Brussels," Nick said. "The security setup for a banking consortium there has been breached."

"Brussels. For how long?"

If she'd asked for her leave to start earlier, she could have gone with him.

"I don't know, a couple of days. I'll call you. I've got to run if I'm going to make the flight." He hung up.

Ashley held the silent receiver for a moment, then replaced it. So much for sharing her news at dinner. It'd keep, of course, until the next time they spoke.

But she wanted to tell him today face-to-face.

Returning early from lunch, Ashley dialed the manager of the new apartment building. She could at least see if he was amenable to their bringing things over early. Even if it cost a bit extra, it'd help make moving easier.

"I still don't have the signed lease," the man said when Ashley identified herself and made her request.

"But it was signed a couple of weeks ago. I signed it and gave it to Nick. He would have mailed it the next day."

Had it gone astray in the mail?

"I don't have it. Did you keep a copy of the signed papers?" Mr. Douglas asked.

She didn't know if Nick had or not. And until he called from Brussels, she couldn't ask.

"I'll check and call you back."

He'd call tonight when she got home from work. She'd ask him then and call the landlord in the morning.

"Actually, you'll need to let me know soon, I have others interested in the apartment, you know. I expected the signed lease back before now."

"My husband's out of town. As soon as I hear from him, I'll ask. I'll call you no later than tomorrow morning, Mr. Douglas."

What had Nick done with the lease? If he hadn't kept a copy, would the man wait until Nick returned so they could sign a new one? She didn't want to lose that apartment. It was perfect.

Ashley left work early, determined to be home when Nick called.

After changing into comfortable clothes, she went to his desk to see if he'd kept a copy of the signed papers. Rummaging around, she stopped suddenly when she found the original lease. Her signature was clearly on one line.

Nick had not signed.

For a moment she felt stunned.

The paperwork had arrived the day after she'd told him about the baby.

He hadn't signed it.

Sinking on the sofa, Ashley stared at the form, as if it could give her answers.

Why hadn't he signed and returned the lease?

Ashley waited until eleven o clock before going to bed. Nick hadn't called.

The next day she told her assistant to be sure to put Nick through if he phoned.

He did not.

Late in the afternoon, she called Aste to ask for Nick's

location. His secretary didn't know where he was staying, but gave Ashley the number for the bank. Unfortunately it was after hours in Brussels. She doubted Nick, or anyone else for that matter, would be at the bank.

Ashley rose early the next morning and called the bank. After endless attempts to locate him, she finally had to leave a message with one of the clerical workers who spoke English.

Twenty minutes later Nick called.

"Ashley, is there an emergency? I'm right in the middle of something."

"I found the lease to the new apartment on your desk. The landlord said he needed it back right away or he's going to let someone else have our apartment. What's going on, Nick?"

She would not scream her frustration nor voice her greatest fear. Was he regretting their marriage? Regretting their baby? Was he already making plans to leave?

She heard his sigh over the lines.

"We need to talk, but now isn't a good time," he said.

Her heart stopped for a second, then began to race.

She said the same thing on Sunday, but now she didn't want to hear what he had to say. She wanted him to tell her he loved her, that they would stand together through everything and face the future as a couple forever.

"When is a good time?" she asked carefully, afraid she would dissolve in a heap if she didn't hold on tightly to her emotions.

"Not when I'm in the middle of a critical job, that's for sure," he snapped.

"Did you have any intention of telling me you didn't sign the lease? I've been packing, planning to move. When were you going to say something–the morning of the move?"

Her voice rose. She was getting angry. She wanted to stay cool, collected. Even more, she wanted some answers.

"I can't talk from here. I'll call you later."

"You said that Monday and didn't call. When are you coming back?"

"I don't know yet."

She wanted to rage in frustration. Why had he accepted this assignment? Why wasn't he home when she needed him?

"I want some reassurances," she said.

Reassurances for the future. Reassurances he would stay the course. Reassurances he loved her.

"I can't give you any right now," he said and hung up.

Gripping the receiver tightly, she blinked back sudden tears.

He couldn't give her any reassurances?

She loved him. She married him planning to spend the rest of her life with him.

But *he couldn't give her any reassurances.*

Ashley went through the motions of daily life over the next few days. She didn't call Nick again, waiting in vain for him to phone. When Friday afternoon came around and she hadn't heard a word, she called Aste Technologies, asking for Dex.

"Hey, Ashley, what's up?" he asked when he came on the line.

"Do you know when Nick's coming home?" she asked.

"Isn't he home yet?" Dex asked.

"Not that I know of. He was in Brussels."

"He handled that in two days. Finished up Wednesday, I

know because he had some tasks he handed off to one of the techs here to handle. He can make computers do things even their inventors never thought of. He put a firewall in place that will still be working when we are long gone, I expect. But he was done on Wednesday. I thought he headed for home. Now that you mention it, he didn't come in today and I expected him. Hold on, I'll check with his secretary."

Ashley waited, already suspecting the worse.

"Sorry, Ashley, she took a few days since he'd be gone. The temp doesn't know anything. I expect we'll see him when he shows up."

She heard the perplexity in Dex's voice.

"I guess that applies to me as well," she said. "Thanks for the info."

Why hadn't Nick come home?

The weekend proved lonely. Ashley cleaned, did laundry and shopped for groceries. She slept when she could. Napping helped pass the time, however, then she wasn't sleepy at bedtime. She tossed and turned, trying to rest, but worrying far into the night.

She checked the answering machine a dozen times a day in case he called. Nothing. Kept her phone charged every second.

She baked cookies on Sunday afternoon, not wanting to be far from the phone. She was getting worried now about a possible accident. Surely someone would have notified her if that was the case, but what if he'd been mugged and injured with no identification?

The scenario that played itself out the most, however, was his walking away to a new life. He hadn't bargained for a baby.

Hadn't been thrilled with the news when she'd told him.

When the apartment phone rang, she ran for it.

"Hello?"

"Hi, it's Dex, heard from Nick yet?"

"No."

Disappointment washed through her.

"I spoke with one of the managers at the bank in Brussels early this morning. He drove Nick to the airport himself on Wednesday afternoon. He should have landed in New York Wednesday evening. I've got people checking in New York in case there was an accident or something."

"Thanks, Dex. Um, would he have gone somewhere else? Instead of coming home, I mean. Was there another problem or something he might have gone to check out?"

"Not that I know about. Tony's working on it as well. We'll find him, Ashley."

"If he wants to be found," she murmured.

"What?"

"Nothing. I appreciate your letting me know. I'll call you if he calls here."

She hung up and sat back on the chair. Granted she hadn't known Nick long, but he was too honorable to just disappear. He wouldn't leave his friends and partners in the lurch.

Nor was he the type to walk away without a word to her. He'd tell her to her face the marriage wasn't what he wanted and ask her to leave.

She glanced around. She'd never felt fully comfortable in the apartment. Or was it she never felt fully comfortable in the marriage?

She and Darrell had been sweethearts for years, yet he'd run out on her without a qualm.

How much easier would it be for Nick to leave without the years of shared experiences to bind them together?

By Monday morning Ashley was furious.

Nick had better have a whale of an excuse for not calling and letting her know where he was. She refused to be treated like this. Either he keep her informed where he was when he traveled or she'd be the one to end their short-lived marriage.

When she reached work, she discovered her secretary was out sick right when she needed her most in order to wind up some matters in preparation for her leave of absence.

Ashley began to jot down notes for the different accountants who would pick up portions of her workload while she was gone. She wished Stacy had been in, it would have made the day go easier.

As she worked her way steadily through the accounts, she began to wonder if she should bother. If she and Nick weren't going to stay together, then there was no reason to take a leave of absence.

In fact, she needed to work as much as she could in order to have some money saved for the first few months of the baby's life when she wouldn't work.

The thought of being a solo parent again tore at her heart. She knew Michelle had missed a lot with no father figure in her life as a child. If only her parents had been more forgiving or Darrell had at least kept in touch.

Would Nick want anything to do with his son or daughter? Or would he be too busy saving the computers of the world to worry about the child he'd help create?

She'd just changed into comfortable clothes that evening when the apartment phone rang. Hope instantly rose.

"Ashley?" It was Dex.

"Yes?"

"We heard from Nick. Actually, we heard last Thursday, but we had a temporary clerical worker who took the message and it got buried in some other paperwork. He said he had some personal business to take care of and he'd call. Told her to let his wife know. I guess he thought she'd find someone to relay the message, but she apparently just jotted it on a slip of paper and forgot about it."

"That's all, some personal business?"

"So he said."

"Like what?"

"I haven't a clue." Dex hesitated a moment. "You know his uncle's dead. He has no other family he keeps in contact with, so I'm not sure what he meant. It was our screw up, sorry for all the worry on your end."

At least he wasn't in an accident.

"He should have called you directly," Dex said.

"Maybe he was short on time."

She wasn't going to reveal the difficulties they were facing to Dex, no matter how close he was to Nick.

"If he calls again, we'll let you know right away. Sorry for the delay."

So Nick had at least tried to reassure her about his delay. Not that taking care of personal business meant much.

And where was he that he couldn't use his phone? He'd made a big deal of her keeping hers charged. He could have called.

All worry now turned to anger. How dare he put her through so much for naught. If he wanted to try for the long haul, they really did need to sit down and talk and one of the first things she would demand is he keep in contact.

The next morning she left for work early and plowed through all her accounts. She took a quick lunch, then distributed the folders and notes she'd made all morning. Her desk was the cleanest it had ever been. Some of her co-workers commented on her plans, wishing they could take time off to visit some of the world's capitals. She smiled, trying to maintain a calm demeanor when her stomach was in turmoil and her anger was barely kept in check.

When the phone rang around three, she picked up, wishing again Stacy had not been out ill today.

"Mom?" It was Michelle, and she sounded as if she were crying.

"Yes, honey. What is it?"

Had she failed an exam?

"Mom, can you come? Charlie's dead."

10

Ashley willed the taxi to go faster, even though traffic was heavy. She knew the driver was doing his best, but her child needed her and she wanted to be there instantly.

Charlie dead, how could that be? He was only twenty-one years old. He had his whole life ahead of him. Only, apparently no longer.

Michelle must be devastated. Ashley wanted to push against the seat in front of her in hopes of pushing the cab to go faster, to get to her daughter.

Endless minutes later the cab pulled in front of Michelle's apartment building near the university. Ashley flung some money his way and dashed out and into the building.

Seconds later she knocked on the door.

Michelle threw it open, tears tracking down her cheeks.

Ashley was vaguely aware of two men who rose when she entered, but her concern was for her daughter. She took Michelle into her arms, holding her tightly, feeling her own tears come.

"What happened?" she asked, as Michelle sobbed against her shoulder.

"He was killed in an accident," she wailed, sobbing harder.

"Ma'am," one of the men said.

Ashley looked over, recognizing the Navy uniforms.

"I'm sorry we had to bring such bad news," the taller man said.

He hardly looked old enough to wear the double bars on his shoulder.

"What happened?" she asked them, holding her daughter tightly.

"It was a freak shipboard accident. He and three other sailors were killed when ordnance was mis-loaded and misfired. His body's being sent home for burial. It'll be here in two days."

He held out a manila envelope.

"The ship was still in San Diego," Ashley said, stunned anew by the news. Trying to take it in. "Wasn't it?"

"No, ma am. Out on maneuvers. On behalf of the Captain and the entire United States Navy you have our condolences."

He offered the manila envelop again.

"This has all the information you need—arrival time of the body, who to contact to coordinate the funeral. Insurance matters. Who to contact with any questions you have that we can't answer. Do you have any questions for us now?"

Ashley reached for it, and nodded, brushing her own tears away with the back of her hand.

She couldn't let Michelle go long enough to do much more. Her heart ached for her baby girl. She and Charlie hadn't been married three months.

"I don't know. I can't think. I never expected anything like this."

"I'm sorry, ma'am. If it's any consolation, all the men died instantly, no suffering."

Ashley nodded.

It might help in the future to know he hadn't suffered. But to be twenty one and dead, she couldn't take it in.

"If there's nothing else?" the man asked.

There were a million questions—how had this happened? Who all had died? Why? What was her daughter to do with the rest of her life? Who sent mere boys into maneuvers with faulty equipment? How could any of this be happening?

But the man in uniform wouldn't have the answers.

"No. There's nothing."

"Our sincerest condolences," he said formally.

When they'd left, Ashley moved with Michelle to the sofa.

"Oh, Mom, I can't believe it. He's never going to come home. We're never going to build a life together, get a house, have kids. I'd even support his wish to stay in the Navy if he'd been here," she cried, clutching Ashley as if she'd never let go.

"I know honey. I know."

She felt inadequate to deal with all this. What could she do?

She wished Nick were with her. He might have some suggestions. If nothing else, he'd offer support. She needed someone to lean on.

"The Stratford's need to be told. The Navy notified me as next of kin. They have to know. Poor Phyllis. She dotes on Charlie. Doted," Michelle said, tears streaming down her cheeks.

Ashley's tears welled again.

Michelle obviously couldn't tell them.

She'd have to.

Was there anything worse than a mother losing a child? Charlie was the only child Phyllis and Samuel had. This would be devastating news.

Ashley instinctively rested her hand on her swelling stomach.

"I'll call her now. She needs to know," Ashley said.

Michelle told her where the phone number was, and Ashley went to dial, remembering Charlie coming over after school to see Michelle. Remembering the times they'd fought and made up. Remembered the plans they'd made, and the small wedding they'd had so recently.

He'd been far too young to die. And Michelle was much too young to be a widow. They should have had their entire lives ahead of them.

Ashley asked to speak to Samuel when Phyllis answered. He wasn't home Phyllis replied. Ashley couldn't think for a moment, then said she had a tax question for him, unwilling to give Phyllis the news when she was home alone. She asked him to call as soon as he came in.

Then she went to prepare hot, sweet tea for herself and Michelle. There'd be so much to do over the next few days. But first, the initial shock needed to be dealt with.

Michelle stopped crying, listlessly accepting the tea when it was ready.

"I don't know what to do," she said sadly.

"We'll take it one step at a time. The Stratfords will want to be involved in the funeral plans, so we'll wait until they know before planning anything."

"I talked to him last week, when I was in the midst of taking finals. He said they were going to sea for a few weeks, a shakedown cruise or something."

"The Navy officer said it was a freak accident. No one expected anything like this," Ashley said, wishing more than ever that Nick was here to help her deal with this.

She ached for her daughter and the Stratfords.

"He didn't even ask after my finals," Michelle said. "I had to tell him I was taking them. It seems so petty now, but I was upset my finals weren't as important to him as going to his next assignment."

She started to cry again.

"Honey, he was a man, doing a man's job. He was focused on that. You were important to him. He loved you for a long time. Always remember that."

"The call was too short," Michelle mumbled.

"If he'd known he wasn't going to get another chance to call, I'm sure he'd have stayed on the line for hours," Ashley said gently.

There was something to be said for not knowing when the end was coming.

"Maybe. But I don't know how I feel. Not very married. We only had a few nights together, you know. He was down in Monterey almost the entire time since we got married. We never got to do husband and wife things like shopping together. We were going to do all that when he got back. Now we never will."

"I know. I'm so sorry, sweetie."

Ashley would do anything to ease the pain her daughter was going through. She didn't know of anything that would help.

Michelle rose and paced the small room.

Nothing would ever be the same for her. Ashley's heart ached for her daughter.

Nick opened the apartment. He was dog-tired, but more convinced of what he needed to do than he'd been in a long time. It wouldn't be easy, but he had no other choice.

"Ashley?"

The quiet in the apartment indicated he was alone. He'd called from the airport, but no one had seen her in the office since about noon and her secretary was out sick.

And she wasn't answering her cell.

He took his suitcase into the bedroom. She wasn't napping in their bed, which is what he'd been hoping for.

Taking a quick shower to freshen up, he dressed casually and went back into the living room. There was no note.

Of course not, she hadn't known he was coming home today. Hadn't even gotten his message about his visit to Sambo until this morning.

Dex had apologized a dozen times, but it didn't make it easier. What had Ashley thought when she hadn't heard from him in days?

If Sambo hadn't lived in the hills of Virginia, he could have used his cell and called out after that thunderstorm had knocked out the power and phone lines. Told her of the flash floods that had made roads impassable for days.

It had taken the local phone company until last night to get telephone service restored. He'd stayed as long as he could to help clear the roads, worked with the small town in getting its computers back up once power was back and retrieving as much data as he could from the damaged machines. Lightening and computers should never mix.

He'd thought Ashley knew he was fine. Instead, she must have been sick with worry when she hadn't heard from him in a week.

"So where is she now?" he said aloud, dialing her office again.

No luck. No one knew where she was.

He tried Dex again, but he hadn't heard from Ashley since that morning.

He dialed Michelle's cell number, but only got voice mail.

Who were Ashley's friends? She'd spoken about an Abbie and a Marian, but he couldn't remember their last names. Rummaging around her things, he didn't find an address book. Probably still at her old apartment.

He saw the lease to the apartment they had picked together on the kitchen counter. He needed to talk to her about that. He should have done so already, but he'd been running scared.

Heck of a thing for a man to admit to his wife. The thought of a baby had scared the life out of him. He wasn't father material, had never pictured himself as a father.

He tried Michelle's apartment. The phone rang until the machine picked up. He left a brief message and hung up. Nothing to do but wait.

And waiting was never something he was good at.

He went through the mail, keeping an eye on the phone as if that would help it ring.

He got something to eat and fixed a huge pot of coffee. He was tired, but nothing he couldn't handle. Flying in from the East Coast wasn't like coming home from Europe.

It was after seven when he tried Michelle's phone again. Still no answer.

Impatient and worried, he headed out. He'd swing by Ashley's old apartment. Maybe she was packing. Though he doubted it. Knowing he hadn't signed the lease, Ashley probably had given up on the move.

For a moment he wondered if she'd given up on him and moved back to her old place.

He drove the few blocks and was startled to see the lights on. He hadn't truly expected that.

Finding a parking place proved almost impossible. He was tempted to leave the car in the middle of the road and run up to her apartment, demanding to know why she was there instead of their place.

He found a spot about two blocks away. The walk back did nothing but fuel his anger. He'd been waiting for hours, had she been here all along? What was she doing?

He knocked on the door, annoyed she hadn't even given him a key to her place. Her old place, he corrected himself.

Ashley opened the door, shocked to see him. But it was nothing to the shock he experienced seeing her.

"Ashley, what's wrong?"

She looked awful. Her eyes were swollen and blotchy. She didn't have on a speck of make up, and her hair was pulled back as if to keep it out of her face with no regard for style.

"Nick? What are you doing here?"

"I came for you."

"Oh, Nick, Charlie's dead."

She burst into tears.

He stepped inside and drew her into his arms.

"Oh, sweetheart, I didn't know. When did it happen? I would have come instantly if I'd known."

"You're here now, that's good," she said, leaning against him. "We just found out this afternoon. It's so awful."

He turned her slightly and picked her up, carrying her to the sofa where he sat with her in his lap.

"Tell me," he urged, holding her close.

"Michelle's asleep at last. We came home because –"

She stopped and looked at him, her eyes full of worry and sadness.

"Because this is your home, yours and Michelle's. And comfort is what she needs now," he said.

His place had never been hers. Would never be hers. He knew that now.

She nodded, her tears slowing.

"I didn't know you were back," she said, leaning her head against his shoulder wearily.

"I got in this afternoon. I tried calling you at work, but you weren't there. I didn't know you didn't know where I was."

"Michelle called about three. I went straight to her apartment, but we didn't want to stay there. The Stratfords were devastated. I had to tell Samuel. The Navy notified Michelle. I knew they'd be heartbroken. How horrible is it to lose a child? I don't know how they will bear it."

"What happened?"

Three o clock? He'd been at the apartment by four o clock. He could have been with her all these hours.

He listened while Ashley disjointedly told him what she knew. He didn't fully understand where Charlie had been, but did it matter? The fact was the young man was dead and Nick's stepdaughter was a widow at nineteen.

Charlie's parents had lost their only child.

His wife was distraught, which couldn't be good for her or the baby.

And he hadn't been there when she'd needed him most.

She pushed back.

"I need to wash my face again."

She rose and went down the short hall to the bathroom. He heard the water running. Feeling frustrated, he rose and went to the kitchen. The tea kettle was on the stove. Cups were in the sink. Remnants of a meal were still on the counter, little eaten.

He began to clear off the dishes, stacking them in the sink, putting away the food. He heard her join him. She'd pulled a sweatshirt over her clothes. Probably for the residual shock since it was not particularly cool in the apartment.

"I can do those," she said dully.

"I can manage. Sit and talk to me. Tell me what you've decided for the funeral."

She looked at him, a flare of anger showing.

"Where have you been? I've been out of my mind with worry, no word from you in a week. We didn't exactly end on a pleasant note in our last call which by the way was initiated from me. Would you ever have called?"

"I left a message," he said quietly.

He turned off the water and turned to face her, leaning against the counter.

"How dare you waltz back in as if you'd only gone to the store."

"I had some things to see to. I wanted to–"

"Mom?" Michelle appeared in the door. "Oh, hi Nick. I guess you heard?" she asked.

"I'm so sorry, Michelle," he said, taking in her appearance. Gone was the vibrant happy young woman he was used to seeing. Her eyes were dulled from tears. She moved as if she were eighty instead of almost twenty.

"Yeah, me, too."

She went to sit beside Ashley.

"Can't sleep?" Ashley asked drawing her against her.

She shook her head.

"Want me to warm up this food?" Nick asked.

He wasn't sure what to do with two weepy females, but he'd try something.

He hadn't known Charlie well, but he couldn't believe the young man was dead.

She shook her head.

"I don't want anything but to be with Mom."

Ashley reached out and brushed her fingers against Michelle's cheek.

"It'll get better with time, honey. I know it doesn't seem like it now, but it will. I promise."

"It's getting through the now that's so hard," Michelle replied.

Nick felt shut out. The two had a bond he'd never be a part of. They were a family.

He was the outsider who had married Ashley. Had the deck been stacked against them from the beginning?

He finished cleaning the kitchen, trying to ignore the boxes stacked against the far wall. Ashley had been preparing to move and he'd been stalling about making that final decision and signing the lease.

What now?

He turned and leaned against the counter. The two women sat silently watching him.

"Want to go into the other room where it's more comfortable?" he asked.

They shrugged almost in unison and rose, walking into the living room. Sitting side by side on the sofa, Michelle then leaned against Ashley. For a moment Nick could see a little girl, trusting in her mother, the only parent she knew.

At least her childhood had been with Ashley, not the crusty old man who had raised him. Raised him, but not taught him how to be part of a family.

Nick felt as if this was a test. If he passed, he'd be allowed to make a niche for himself with them. If he failed, he'd be back on his own, only it would be worse this time because he'd known Ashley and had a glimpse of what life with her could be.

"You needn't stay, Nick," Ashley said, leaning back and closing her eyes. "We'll be fine."

"You're my wife, of course I'm staying."

Was she trying to send him away? Didn't she want him to stay?

"Now's a fine time to remember. Where have you been?"

He glanced at Michelle. She was looking at him, but he had a feeling she wasn't really seeing him.

"I had some things to work through," he said, sitting in the chair opposite her.

He didn't want to have this discussion with a third party present. But he wasn't leaving, either. Not before he and Ashley had cleared things up.

"Where there were no phones?" she asked skeptically.

"Actually, that's about it. I went to see an old friend. He and his wife live in the mountains of Virginia. Unfortunately there's no cell reception. And there was a storm. Power lines and phone lines were knocked out. I thought you got my message on Thursday."

"I didn't."

"I know, now."

"You didn't sign the lease."

He shook his head.

"Should I leave?"

Michelle asked, looking back and forth between her mother and Nick.

"No," Ashley said.

"Maybe it would be better," Nick said simultaneously.

Ashley glared at him.

"She just lost her husband. Maybe I'm losing mine."

Nick felt sucker punched.

"What are you talking about?"

"I know you don't want a baby, you've said so often enough."

"I have never said it once."

"You have."

"What I've said more than once is I can't picture myself as a father. Which is true. Actually, I never pictured myself as a husband, but you changed that. And now we're having our baby."

"And you're thrilled," she said sarcastically.

"Actually, thrilled isn't quite how I'd put it. Scared silly id more like it."

Ashley looked at him. "Of a baby?"

He nodded.

"I have never pictured myself as a father mainly because

I don't have a clue how to be a father."

"Being around goes a long way in my book," Michelle murmured. "Mine never was."

"Babies don't know anything when they're born," Ashley said. "Whoever they get is usually fine with them. And you don't become an instant knowledgeable father or mother. It takes time. I was so scared when Michelle was born. Heck, I still don't know what to do all the time, look at this situation. But I wouldn't trade her for anything in the world."

"You're a great mother," Michelle said, hugging Ashley. She looked over at Nick.

"At least your baby will have his or her father. Just love the kid a lot and you'll be fine."

"I'll try to remember that," he said, tilting his head slightly and looking at Ashley.

If Michelle wasn't in the room, he'd sweep up his wife and take her to bed to try to erase the sadness that permeated her being. He hated knowing he'd caused some of it.

Ashley studied him, as if seeking an explanation for what had to be a reversal of what she thought.

"I've had time to think about us, about the changes a baby will bring," he said. "And I'm okay with everything."

"Since when?" she asked.

"Since spending the weekend with Sambo and his wife and three kids."

"Who's Sambo? What kind of name is Sambo?"

"Sam Bond. He and Dex and I went to college together. He went back east, settled in a town in western Virginia, got married and has two girls and a boy. They're terrific kids."

Ashley and Michelle both stared at him.

"Cut me a break. I've never been around children before. I don't even have any friends who have kids, except for Sam. And he lives three thousand miles away. You know my background. Did you think I'd ever dream of some day having a son or daughter depending on me? What kind of father would I be?"

"I think you will be a wonderful father," Michelle said softly.

He was surprised at that.

"You do?"

She nodded, smiling slightly.

The thought shouldn't please him so much, but it did.

Ashley smiled.

"If you could see your expression."

"That means a lot, Michelle. Thanks."

Ashley's eyes filled with tears suddenly.

"If you're staying, that is," she said.

He shook his head, totally bemused.

"What do you mean if I'm staying? Of course I am, I just needed to fix a few things in my head. It's a done deal. I spoke with Dex and Tony this afternoon. No more travel for me for at least a year. We'll have this baby together."

"No travel?" Ashley asked. "But that's what you do."

"No, it's what I did."

"I thought you didn't sign the lease because you wanted to be in London, not San Francisco. And maybe wanted to be there unencumbered, without a wife and baby."

"I didn't sign the lease because I wondered if we needed a larger place for our new baby and to have a room for our daughter and her husband to visit."

"Oh," Ashley said.

"Maybe now more than ever we'll need a larger place. Where will you live, Michelle? You are welcome to be with us."

Ashley looked at Michelle. Where indeed?

"Once the funeral's over, I'll go back to school to finish this year if possible. I'll have to get a job. Thanks for the offer, but I can't live with you and Mom," Michelle said slowly.

"We'd love to have you," Nick said, glancing at Ashley for agreement.

She nodded, her smile almost as happy as he'd ever seen it. Only a tinge of sadness lingered.

He'd do anything to have her smile be as radiant as it had been on their wedding day.

Michelle looked between them again, then rose.

"I need to go to bed. Thanks for being here, Nick. And thanks for the offer."

When Michelle left, Ashley spoke softly,

"Thank you. That was special to invite her to live with us."

"I meant it."

"I know you did. It surprised me, however."

"Why?"

"I thought you'd come to tell me you were leaving. That our marriage was over," Ashley said slowly.

11

Ashley was gratified at the look on Nick's face. Obviously she'd been wrong.

"Well, you didn't sign the lease, you were gone without telling me where, you didn't talk to me, you went off with your friends, and you kept saying," she trailed off as he rose purposefully and advanced toward her.

"I never said I didn't want the baby."

"You changed when I told you about it."

"You caught me totally by surprise. I do admit I've been angry you didn't quit your job and travel with me. Especially when circumstances changed."

"I was afraid. Afraid you'd leave me and I'd be homeless and destitute."

"That doesn't make sense. I'm never leaving you."

"We married so fast. I thought that if we couldn't do what we planned, you'd leave."

"I've told you before, I'm not your first husband. I would never leave you. Don't you have a clue how important you are to me?"

She shook her head slowly.

"Take a leap of faith, Ashley. Believe me when I say I will never leave you. Not a baby, your job or anything else is going to separate us."

"It's too late."

"What's too late?"

"For me to quit and for us to travel."

"Why?"

She blinked.

"It should be obvious. Before long I'll look like a beached whale. I'll need to be no farther than fourteen feet from a bathroom. I'll have the energy of a slug. Won't be able to tie my shoes, much less travel to Europe or the Far East."

"So?"

He shrugged, sitting beside her, putting his arm around her shoulder, as if to anchor her next to him.

"We'll deal with that when the situation arises. Did you know Sam and his wife go hiking on the Appalachian Trail every year, pregnant, infants and all?"

"What?"

"I've learned a lot these last few days. Pregnant women can do whatever they want including visiting foreign locales. We'll have to make sure we're home in plenty of time for the delivery, but otherwise, if you want, we can still take our trips. I've told Dex I'm not taking any business trips until this time next year. But that doesn't mean you and I can't take some just for the adventure. I'm not spending days away from my wife. I want to see all the changes the baby brings. And be here when he is born. When he's old enough, we'll be ready to take up traveling again."

"You love to travel, that's the best part of your job," she said.

"I do like to travel."

He laced his fingers with hers.

"But over the last couple of months, I've discovered, I like being with you even more. If we never leave San Francisco again, I'll be happy with you. I never had anyone to share my life with–no one who wanted me just for me before. I realized in Stockholm and Brussels how little visiting those places means these days when you aren't with me."

"I requested a leave of absence at work. I was going to tell you the day you left for Brussels. I'm ready to go with you," she said, overwhelmed with the burst of love that filled her heart.

He tugged her closer, and brushed his lips over her fingers.

"So we'll travel as time permits until the baby's born. We can revisit our plan to settle temporarily in London. Think how worldly our child will be as he grows up visiting Madrid or Brussels or Tokyo."

"He?"

She latched on to the one thing she could, her mind a whirl with the possibilities as Nick presented them.

"Or she. Or they."

"They?"

"We don't want this child to grow up lonely, do we? I was an only, you were, Michelle was until now. Didn't we all long for siblings?"

"You want more children?"

Ashley's eyes were wide in surprise.

"First of all, I want you. Then, yes. I think I might want a family full of kids. If we ever decide to settle down we can get a house. But in the meantime, a large apartment, that someone can watch for us while we're traveling, will do."

"So you want to stay married," Ashley wanted that clearly stated.

"I meant what I said. You are more important than anything else I have or hope to ever have. I would do anything for you, Ashley. I wish you believed that."

He kissed her, long and deep. She came up for air and smiled at him.

"I guess I can try," she said.

"For the next fifty or sixty years. Give me a chance to show you I'm not some guy who's going to walk out on you. I'm in this for life. Our life together. Believe it, sweetheart," he said.

"I do."

"Maybe this life we'll share isn't going to be the way we thought when we got married a couple of months ago. But that doesn't mean it won't be even better," he said.

"I wanted to be footloose and fancy-free. To travel and see the world. To go sailing, and exploring and learn a new language."

"And you can. We can make it work however we want to. As long as we're together as a family."

"I love you, Nick," she said.

"I love you, Ashley. And I always will."

"You do?"

He frowned. "You needn't sound so surprised."

"You never told me before."

She turned slightly, framing his face with both her palms.

"Tell me again, look right at me and tell me."

"I love you, Ashley Carstairs," he said solemnly, then kissed her.

When he ended the kiss, he rested his forehead against hers.

"How could you doubt my love?"

"At first I didn't, but then you grew so distant after I told you about the baby."

"It was a complete surprise. I was running scared. And until I read that baby book on the plane ride home, I wasn't sure how much you and I could do exactly."

He trailed off.

Ashley laughed, her heart filled to overflowing.

"We can do anything we want, right up until the last couple of weeks."

"I'm all for that, then," he said, tucking a strand of hair behind her ear. "I meant what I said about Michelle. She might want to live with us for a little while, and that's fine with me."

"Oh, Nick, thank you. We can let the situation settle a bit for Michelle before making any long-range decisions. She may truly wish to be on her own for a while."

"I can't believe her young husband's gone. I don't know how to handle that either. Life with you, sweetheart, is not at all like I thought it would be."

"It'll be okay, won't it?"

She still wanted assurances. He'd promised to love her forever. She figured that'd just be about the right amount of time.

"It'll be better than okay. It'll be the greatest adventure we'll ever have. Now, what do you say we go to bed. I want to make love to my wife," Nick said.

She rose and held out her hands to him.

"I want that, too. I need to feel loved and wanted and

alive. I'm sad about Charlie. My heart aches for my daughter. But there is nothing more I can do for her right now. Something life-affirming would be so welcomed."

He swung her up into his arms and headed down the short hall to the narrow bed that would be theirs for the night.

"I will affirm our life together every day. I love you, Ashley. You and however many babies we have," Nick said as a vow.

The radiant smile she gave him was every bit as good as the one on their wedding day.

Epilogue

"Now close your eyes and toss in the coin," Nick said, holding Ashley's shoulders gently.

She did so and then opened her eyes, smiling at the Trevi Fountain. "So now we'll for sure come back."

She took a couple of photographs with her phone, and turned to Nick.

"So the legend goes," he said.

"We have to, we haven't seen everything yet," Ashley said. "And while I've loved every moment, I am looking to returning home later today. We've done a lot of walking the last few days."

"A short hop to London and we'll be in our own bed tonight."

She slipped her hand in the crook of his arm as they ambled away from the famous Roman fountain.

"Michelle must feel like she's sharing our visit with all the pictures you've sent," Nick said as they walked toward their hotel to get their luggage and then head for the airport.

"I still feel badly she returned alone to San Francisco when it was time for classes to begin again. She loved being in London with us."

"She said finishing her degree was what she wanted. She can still join us whenever she wants."

"Finishing college became her focus after the funeral. She wants to move forward with her life. I only wish we weren't so far away."

"Having second thoughts about living in London?" Nick asked.

"No. I love our flat. We decided to do what we talked about. Charlie's sudden death was a reminder none of us is guaranteed endless days. Now's the best time for us to live in Europe. Look at all the short hops we've made to other countries. I'm loving every moment."

After deciding to move to London as they'd once dreamed, they kept Nick's apartment to have a place in San Francisco. But for the foreseeable future, London was home. They'd made the most of the time before pregnancy became too awkward to visit different areas in England. Then a trip to Paris had been the next adventure.

Their Roman holiday was coming to a close. The late September weather was still lovely, without being too hot to find walking around the old city a problem.

"What did you like best?" she asked.

"Watching you be enchanted by everything you saw," Nick answered promptly.

She laughed.

"It's too exciting not to be enchanted."

"Maybe, but I've seen a lot of this old city before. Seeing it again with you makes it that much more special. I'm glad we came. We'll come again."

"But probably not before the baby's born," Ashley said.

"Not if Madrid's our next destination. There's plenty to do to finish getting the flat fixed up, getting the rest of the things for the baby and exploring more of London. We won't be bored."

Ashley looked at him, stopping to face him.

"I'm never bored with you. These have been the most exciting and special months of my life. I love you."

He cupped her face with his hand and gave her a quick kiss. "I love you, sweetheart. I really hit the jackpot in Lake Tahoe when you knocked my coins to the floor. Who knew I'd become the world's biggest winner that day?"

If you liked **Her Not So Empty Nest,**
you may enjoy **Love Is All The Sweeter** and
The Talmadge Sisters box sets.

If you enjoyed **Her Not So Empty Nest,**
please consider leaving a review.

More books by Barbara McMahon

Golden Gate Romance Series
Billionaire's Betrothal
Dakota's Hero
Finding a Wife for Tanner
Love Times Three
Her Not So Empty Nest

Cowboys of Wildcat Creek
Valentine's Cowboy Rescue
Shelly and the Cowboy
Kristi's Cowboy Hero
Holly's Reluctant Cowboy
A Cowboy for Eliza

Sweet Reunion Romance Collection
Unexpected Reunion
Unpredictable Reunion
Unanticipated Reunion

The Talmadge Sisters
Letters to Caroline
Michelle's Marriage Deal
Trusting Abby

The Harts of Texas Series
Rebel Heart
Tangled Hearts
Reckless Heart

A Sweet Clean Christmas Romance Collection
The Christmas Cop
The Cowboy's Special Christmas
A Soldier's Christmas
A Teaspoon of Mistletoe
The Christmas Locket
A Key West Christmas